PRAISE FOR *Javier Marías*

"Marías is one of the best contemporary writers."
—J. M. Coetzee

"By far Spain's best writer today."   —Roberto Bolaño

"One of the writers who should get the Nobel Prize is Javier Marías."
—Orhan Pamuk

"Stylish, cerebral. . . . Marías is a startling talent. . . . His prose is ambitious, ironic, philosophical and ultimately compassionate."
—*The New York Times*

"It is a rare gift, to be offered a writer who lives in our own time but speaks with the intensity of the past, who comes with the extra richness lent by a foreign history and nonetheless knows our own culture inside out. Yet, strangely, Javier Marías—who is famous in Spain and garlanded with prizes from the rest of Europe—remains almost unknown in America. What are we waiting for?"   —*The New York Times Book Review*

"Javier Marías is one of the greatest living authors. I cannot think of one single contemporary writer that reaches his level of quality. If I had to name one, it would be García Márquez."
—Marcel Reich-Ranicki, *Das Literarische Quartett*

"Javier Marías is such an elegant, witty and persuasive writer that it is tempting simply to quote him at length."
—*The Scotsman*

"A supreme stylist."   —*The Times* (London)

"Marías uses language like an anatomist uses the scalpel to cut away the layers of the flesh in order to lay bare the innermost secrets of that strangest of species, the human being."

—W. G. Sebald

"His prose possesses an exquisite, almost uncanny observation, re-creating moments and moods in hypnotic depth."

—*The Telegraph* (London)

"Javier Marías is a novelist with style. . . . His readers enter, through him, a strikingly and disturbingly foreign world."

—Margaret Drabble

"Marías writes the kind of old-fashioned speculative prose we associate with Proust and Henry James. . . . But he also deals in violence, historical and personal, and in the movie titles, politicians, and brand names and underwear we connect with quite a different kind of writer." —*London Review of Books*

Javier Marías

WHEN I WAS MORTAL

Javier Marías was born in Madrid in 1951. He has published thirteen novels, two collections of short stories, and several volumes of essays. His work has been translated into forty-two languages, in fifty-two countries, and won a dazzling array of international literary awards, including the prestigious Dublin IMPAC award for *A Heart So White*. He is also a highly practiced translator into Spanish of English authors, including Joseph Conrad, Robert Louis Stevenson, Sir Thomas Browne, and Laurence Sterne. He has held academic posts in Spain, the United States, and in Britain, as Lecturer in Spanish Literature at Oxford University.

INTERNATIONAL

WHEN I
WAS MORTAL

STORIES

Javier Marías

Translated from the Spanish
by Margaret Jull Costa

VINTAGE INTERNATIONAL
VINTAGE BOOKS
A DIVISION OF RANDOM HOUSE, INC.
NEW YORK

The translator would like to thank Javier Marías,
Annella McDermott, and Ben Sherriff
for all their help and advice.

M.J.C.

A VINTAGE INTERNATIONAL EDITION, APRIL 2013

Translation copyright © 1999 by Margaret Jull Costa

All rights reserved. Published in the United States by
Vintage Books, a division of Random House, Inc., New York,
and in Canada by Random House of Canada Limited, Toronto.
Originally published in Spain as *Cuando fui mortal* by Editorial Alfaguara,
Madrid, in 1996. Copyright © 1996 by Javier Marías. This translation
originally published in slightly different form in Great Britain
by The Harvill Press, London, in 1999.

The Cataloging-in-Publication data is on file
at the Library of Congress.

Vintage ISBN: 978-0-307-95078-9

www.vintagebooks.com

Printed in the United States of America

CONTENTS

PREFACE

Of the twelve stories that make up this volume, I think eleven were commissioned. That means that I did not have absolute freedom when writing those eleven, especially as regards length. Three pages here, ten pages there, forty or so there, the requests are very varied and one tries to fulfil these requirements as best one can. I know that in two of the stories, I found the limitations constraining, which is why they appear here in expanded form, with the space and rhythm which – once begun – they should have had. As for the rest, including those that fulfilled some other external requirement, I don't think that the commission comprised them in any way, at least not after a time and now that I've grown accustomed to them as they are. You can write an article or a story on commission (though not, in my case, a whole book); sometimes even the subject matter may be given and I see nothing wrong in that as long you manage to make the final product yours and you enjoy writing it. Indeed, I can only write something if I'm enjoying myself and I can only enjoy myself if I find the project interesting. It goes without saying that none of these stories would have been written if I had felt no interest in them. It is perhaps worth reminding those sentimental purists who believe that, in order to sit down in front of the typewriter, you have to experience grandiose feelings such as a creative "need" or "impulse", which are always "spontaneous" or terribly intense, that the majority of the sublime works of art produced over the centuries – especially in painting and music – were the result of commissions or of even more prosaic or servile stimuli.

In the circumstances, however, it may not be out of place to detail briefly how and when these stories were published for the first time and to comment on some of the impositions that soon became absorbed into them and are as much part of the story as any other chosen element. They are arranged in strict chronological order of publication, which does not always coincide with the order in which they were written.

"The Night Doctor" appeared in the magazine *Ronda Iberia* (Madrid, June 1991).

"The Italian Legacy" was published in the literary supplement of the newspaper *El Sol* (Madrid, 6 September, 1991).

"The Honeymoon" appeared in the magazine *Balcón* (special Frankfurt edition, Madrid, October 1991). This story shares the central plot and several paragraphs with a few pages from my novel *Corazón tan blanco*, 1992 (English translation: *A Heart So White*, Harvill, 1995). The scene in question continues in the novel, whereas here it breaks off, allowing a different resolution, which is what makes of the text a story. It's a demonstration of how the same pages may not necessarily be the same pages, as Borges showed, better than anyone, in his story: "Pierre Menard, autor de *El Quijote*" ("Pierre Menard, author of *Don Quixote*").

"Broken Binoculars" was published in the ephemeral magazine *La Capital* (Madrid, July 1992) with the worst printer's error ever perpetrated on one of my texts: they failed to print the first page of my typescript, so that the story was published incomplete and starting abruptly *in media res*. Despite that, it seemed to survive the mutilation. I was asked to write a story with a Madrid setting, although, to be honest, I don't really know what that means.

"Unfinished Figures" appeared in *El País Semanal* (Madrid and Barcelona, 9 August, 1992). On this occasion, the commission was positively sadistic. In a very short space I had to include five elements, which were, if I remember rightly: the sea, a storm, an animal... I've forgotten the other two, proof that they are now completely absorbed into the story.

"Flesh Sunday" appeared in *El Correo Español-El Pueblo Vasco* and in *Diario Vasco* (Bilbao and San Sebastián, 30 August, 1992). In this very short story, the one requirement was, I believe, that it should have a summer setting.

"When I Was Mortal" was published in *El País Semanal* (Madrid and Barcelona, 8 August, 1993).

"Everything Bad Comes back" formed part of the book *Cuentos europeos* (Editorial Anagrama, Barcelona, 1994; published in English as *The Alphabet Garden: European Short Stories*, ed. Pete Ayrton, Serpent's Tail, 1994). It's probably the most autobiographical story I've ever written, as will become clear if you read my article "La muerte de Aliocha Coll" included in *Pasiones pasadas* (Editorial Anagrama, Barcelona, 1991).

"Fewer Scruples" appeared in the free publication *La condición humana* (FNAC, Madrid, 1994). This is one of the two stories I have expanded for this edition, by about fifteen per cent.

"Blood on a spear" was published in instalments by *El País* (27, 28, 29, 30 and 31 August and 1 September 1995). The requirement for this story was that it had to belong more or less to the genre of crime novel or thriller. This is the other story I have since expanded, by about ten per cent.

"In Uncertain Time" was included in the book *Cuentos de fútbol*, ed. Jorge Valdano (Alfaguara, Madrid, 1995). Obviously, the requirement here was that the story should be about football.

Lastly, "No More Love" is published here for the first time, although the story it tells was contained – in compressed form – in an article, "Fantasmas leídos", in my collection *Literatura y fantasma* (Ediciones Siruela, Madrid, 1993). There the story was attributed to a non-existent "Lord Rymer" (in fact, the name of a secondary character in my novel *Todas las almas* [Editorial Anagrama Barcelona, 1989; English translation: *All Souls*, Harvill,

1992], the hard-drinking warden of an Oxford college), supposedly an expert and an investigator of real ghosts, if that is not a contradiction in terms. I didn't like the idea that this short story should remain buried alone in the middle of an article and in almost embryonic form, which is why I have expanded it into this new story. It contains conscious, deliberate and acknowledged echoes of a film and of another story: *The Ghost and Mrs Muir* by Joseph L. Mankiewicz, about which I wrote an article in my book *Vida del fantasma* (El País-Aguilar, Madrid, 1995) and "Polly Morgan" by Alfred Edgar Coppard which I included in my anthology *Cuentos únicos* (Ediciones Siruela, 1989). It's all perfectly above board, and there's no question of trying to deceive anyone, which is why the main character of the story is called quite plainly "Molly Morgan Muir".

These twelve stories were written later than those published in my other volume of short stories, *Mientras ellas duermen* (Editorial Anagrama, Barcelona, 1990). There are still a few scattered elsewhere, written very freely or without any commission: it seems advisable to me, however, that they should either remain in obscurity or else scattered.

November 1995

WHEN I WAS MORTAL

THE NIGHT DOCTOR

For LB, in the present,
And DC, in the past

NOW THAT I know my friend Claudia is a widow – following her husband's death from natural causes – I keep remembering one particular night in Paris six months ago: I had left at the end of a supper party for seven in order to accompany one of the guests home – she had no car, but lived close by, fifteen minutes there and fifteen minutes back. She had struck me as a somewhat impetuous, rather nice young woman, an Italian friend of my hostess Claudia, who is also Italian, and in whose Paris flat I was staying for a few days, as I had on other occasions. It was the last night of my trip. The young woman, whose name I cannot now remember, had been invited for my benefit, as well as to add a little variety to the supper table or, rather, so that the two languages being spoken were more evenly spread.

During the walk, I had to continue muddling through in my fractured Italian, as I had during half the supper. During the other half, I had muddled through in my even more fractured French, and to tell the truth I was fed up with being unable to express myself correctly to anyone. I felt like compensating for this lack, but there would, I thought, be no chance to do so that night, for by the time I got back to the flat, my friend Claudia,

who spoke fairly convincing Spanish, would already have gone
to bed with her ageing giant of a husband, and there would be
no opportunity until the following morning to exchange a few
well-chosen and clearly enunciated words. I felt the stirring of
verbal impulses, but I had to repress them. I switched off during
the walk: I allowed my Italian friend's Italian friend to express
herself correctly in her own language, and I, against my will and
my desire, merely nodded occasionally and said from time to
time: "*Certo, certo,*" without actually listening to what she said,
weary as I was with the wine and worn out by my linguistic
efforts. As we walked along, our breath visible in the air, I noticed
only that she was talking about our mutual friend, which was,
after all, quite normal, since, apart from the supper party for
seven that we had just left, we had nothing much else in common.
Or so I thought. "*Ma certo,*" I kept saying pointlessly, while she,
who must have realized I wasn't listening, continued talking as
if to herself or perhaps out of mere politeness. Until suddenly,
still talking about Claudia, I heard a sentence which I understood
perfectly as a sentence, but not its meaning, because I had understood it unwittingly and completely out of context. "*Claudia
sarà ancora con il dottore,*" was what I thought her friend said. I
didn't take much notice, because we were nearly at her door, and
I was anxious to speak my own language again or at least to be
alone so that I could think in it.

There was someone waiting in the doorway, and she added:
"*Ah no, ecco il dottore,*" or something of the sort. It seems the
doctor had come to see her husband, who had been too ill to
accompany her to the supper party. The doctor was a man of my
age, almost young, and he turned out to be Spanish. That may
have been why we were introduced, albeit briefly (they spoke to
each other in French, my compatriot in his unmistakably Spanish
accent), and although I would have happily stayed there for a

while chatting to him in order to satisfy my longing for some correct verbification, my friend's friend did not invite me in, but instead bade me a hasty goodbye, giving me to understand or saying that Dr Noguera had been there for some minutes waiting for her. My compatriot the doctor was carrying a black case, like the ones doctors used to have, and he had an old-fashioned face, like someone out of the 1930s: a good-looking man, but gaunt and pale, with the fair, slicked-back hair of a fighter pilot. It occurred to me that there must have been many like him in Paris after the Spanish Civil War, exiled Republican doctors.

When I got back to the apartment, I was surprised to see the light still on in the studio, for I had to pass by the door on my way to the guest room. I peered in, assuming that it had been left on by mistake, and was ready to turn it off, when I saw my friend was still up, curled in an armchair, in her nightdress and dressing gown. I had never seen her in her nightdress and dressing gown before, despite, over the years, having stayed at her various apartments each time I went to Paris for a few days: both garments were salmon pink, and very expensive. Although the giant husband she had been married to for six years was very rich, he was also very mean, for reasons of character, nationality or age – a relatively advanced age in comparison with Claudia – and my friend had often complained that he only ever allowed her to buy things to further embellish their large, comfortable apartment, which was, according to her, the only visible manifestation of his wealth. Otherwise, they lived more modestly than they needed to, that is, below their means.

I had had barely anything to do with him, apart from the odd supper party like the one that night, which are perfect opportunities for not talking to or getting to know anyone that you don't already know. The husband, who answered to the strange and ambiguous name of Hélie (which sounded rather feminine to my

ears), I saw as an appendage, the kind of bearable appendage that
many still attractive, single or divorced women have a tendency
to graft onto themselves when they touch forty or forty-five: a
responsible man, usually a good deal older, with whom they share
no interests in common and with whom they never laugh, but
who is, nevertheless, useful to them in their maintaining a busy
social life and organizing suppers for seven as on that particular
night. What struck one about Hélie was his size: he was nearly six
foot five and fat, especially round the chest, a kind of Cyclopean
spinning top poised on two legs so skinny that they looked like
one; whenever I passed him in the corridor, he would always
sway about and hold out his hands to the walls so as to have
something to lean on should he slip; at suppers, of course, he sat
at one end of the table because, otherwise, the side on which he
was installed would have been filled to capacity by his enormous
bulk and would have looked unbalanced, with him sitting alone
opposite four guests all crammed together. He spoke only French
and, according to Claudia, was a leading light in his field – the
law. After six years of marriage, it wasn't so much that my friend
seemed disillusioned, for she had never shown much enthusiasm anyway, but she seemed incapable of disguising, even in the
presence of strangers, the irritation we always feel towards those
who are superfluous to us.

"What's wrong? Still awake?" I said, relieved finally to be able
to express myself in my own language.

"Yes, I feel really ill. The doctor's coming."

"At this hour?"

"He's a night doctor, he's on call. I often have to get him out
at night."

"But what's wrong? You didn't mention anything to me."

Claudia dimmed the lamp that stood by the armchair, as if she
wanted the room to be in darkness before she replied, or else did

not want me to catch some involuntary expression on her face, for our faces, when they speak, are full of involuntary expressions.

"It's nothing, women's problems. But it really hurts when I get it. The doctor gives me an injection to ease the pain."

"I see. And couldn't Hélie learn to do that for you?"

Claudia gave me an unequivocally wary look and lowered her voice to answer that question, though she hadn't lowered it to answer the others.

"No, he can't. His hands shake too much, I don't trust him. If he gave me the injection I'm sure it wouldn't do me any good, or else he'd just get all mixed up and inject something else into me, some poison. The doctor they usually send is very nice and, besides, that's what they're there for, to come to people's apartments in the early hours of the morning. He's Spanish by the way. He'll be here any moment."

"A Spanish doctor?"

"Yes, I think he's from Barcelona. I assume he has French nationality, he must have in order to practise here. He's been here for years."

Claudia had changed her hairstyle since I left the apartment to walk her friend home. Maybe she had merely let her hair down prior to going to bed, but it looked to me as if she had done her hair specially, rather than undone it at the end of the day.

"Do you want me to keep you company while you wait or would you rather be alone if you're in pain?" I asked rhetorically since, having found her still up, I wasn't prepared to go off to bed without satisfying my desire to have a chat and a rest from those other abominable languages and from the wine drunk during the evening. Before she had a chance to reply, I added: "Your friend's very nice. She said her husband was ill; the local doctors are in for a busy night."

Claudia hesitated for a few seconds and it seemed to me that she again looked at me warily, but said nothing. Then she said, this time without looking at me:

"Yes, she's got a husband too; he's even more unbearable than mine. Hers is young, though, just a bit older than her, but she's had him for ten years now and he's just as mean. Like me, she doesn't earn very much with her job, and he even rations out the hot water. Once he used his old bath water to water the plants, which died soon after. When they go out together, he won't even buy her a coffee, they each pay for themselves, so that sometimes she goes without and he has a full afternoon tea. She doesn't earn that much, and he's one of those men who thinks that the person who earns less in a marriage is inevitably taking advantage of the other. He's obsessed with it. He monitors all her phone calls, he's fitted the phone with a device that stops her calling anywhere outside of the city, so that if she wants to speak to her family in Italy she has to go to a public phone box and use coins or a card."

"Why doesn't she leave him?"

Claudia didn't reply at once:

"I don't know; for the same reason I don't, although my situation isn't as bad as hers. I suppose it's true that she does earn less, I suppose she does take advantage of him; I suppose they're right, these men who are obsessed with the money they spend or manage to save with their low-earning wives; but that's what marriage is about, everything has its compensations and it all evens out in the end." Claudia dimmed the light still further, so that we were sitting in almost complete darkness. Her nightdress and dressing gown seemed to glow red, an effect of the growing dark. She lowered her voice still further, to the point where it became a furious whisper. "Why do you think I get these pains, why do you think I have to call a doctor out to give me a sedative? It's just as well it only happens on nights when we give suppers or parties, when he's eaten and drunk and enjoyed himself. When he's seen that others have seen me. He thinks about other men and about their eyes, about what others don't know about, but take for granted or assume, and then he wants to make it reality, not just taken for granted or assumed or unknown. Not imaginary. Then it isn't enough for him just to imagine it." She fell silent for a moment and added: "That great lump of a man is sheer torment."

Although our friendship went back a long way, we had never exchanged this kind of confidence. Not that it bothered me, on the contrary, there's nothing I like more than being privy to such revelations. But I wasn't used to it with her, and I may have blushed a little (not that she would have seen me) and I answered awkwardly, perhaps dissuading her from continuing, the exact opposite of what I wanted:

"I see."

The doorbell went, a feeble ring, just loud enough to be heard, the way you ring at the door of a house where people are already alerted or expecting you to call.

"It's the night doctor," said Claudia.

"I'll leave you then. Goodnight, and I hope you feel better soon."

We left the studio together, she went into the hall and I in the opposite direction, towards the kitchen, where I thought I might read the newspaper for a while before going to bed, for at night the kitchen was the warmest room in the house. Before turning the corner of the corridor that would take me there, though, I paused and looked back towards the front door that Claudia was opening at that very moment, obscuring with her salmon-coloured back the figure of the doctor who had just arrived. I heard her say to him in Spanish: "*Buenas noches*," and all I could see, in the doctor's left hand, sticking out from behind my Italian friend's body, was a bag identical to that carried by the other doctor to whom I had been introduced at the door by her

friend – also Italian – whose name I can't remember. The doctor
must have come by car, I thought.

They closed the front door and walked down the corridor
without seeing me, with Claudia in front, and then I headed for
the kitchen. There I sat down and poured myself a gin (ridiculous, mixing drinks like that) and opened the Spanish paper I
had bought that afternoon. It was from the previous day, but
for me the news was still fresh.

I heard my friend and the doctor go into the children's room,
the children were spending the weekend with other children in
someone else's house. The room was immediately opposite the
kitchen, on the other side of a broad corridor, so, after a few
moments, I moved the chair I was sitting on so that I could just
see the door of the room out of the corner of my eye. The door
was ajar, they had switched on a very dim light, as dim, I said to
myself, as the one that had lit the studio while she and I were
talking and she was waiting. I couldn't see them, I couldn't
hear anything either. I went back to reading my newspaper, but,
after a while, I looked up again because I sensed a presence in
the doorway of the door that stood ajar. And then I saw the
doctor, in profile, holding a syringe in his left hand. I only saw
him for an instant, and since he was standing against the light,
I couldn't see his face. I noticed he was left-handed: it was that
moment when doctors and nurses raise the syringe in the air
and press down the plunger, just a little, to make sure that the
liquid comes out and there's no danger of any blockage or, more
seriously, no danger of injecting air. That's what the nurse,
Cayetano, used to do in my house when I was a child. After
performing this action, the doctor stepped forward and again
disappeared from my field of vision. Claudia must have been
lying down on one of the children's beds, which was probably
where the light was coming from, too faint for me but sufficient

for the doctor. I assumed he would inject her in the bottom.

I returned to my newspaper and a long time passed, too long, before either she or the republican doctor were once again framed in the doorway. Then I had the vague feeling that I was being nosy and it occurred to me that perhaps they were actually waiting for me to go to my room in order to come out and say goodbye. It also occurred to me that, immersed as I had been in reading an article about some sporting controversy, they might have quietly slipped out of the room without my noticing. Trying not to make any noise so as at least not to wake old Hélie, who would have been asleep for some time, I got up to go to bed. Before leaving the kitchen with my newspaper under my arm, I switched off the light, and that switching off of the light and my momentary stillness (the moment before taking a first step down the corridor) coincided with the reappearance in the doorway of the two figures, that of my friend Claudia and that of the night doctor. They paused on the threshold, and from my place in the darkness, I saw them peering in my direction, or so I thought. During that moment, what they saw was the extinguished kitchen light, and since I remained motionless, they probably assumed that I had gone off to my room without their noticing. If I allowed them to believe such a thing, if I, in fact, remained there motionless after seeing them, it was because the doctor, again standing against the light, once more raised the syringe in his left hand, and Claudia, in her nightdress and dressing gown, was clinging onto his other arm as if to instil him with courage by her touch or else restore his composure by her breathing. Thus, arm in arm, bound together by what was about to happen, they moved out of the children's room, and I lost sight of them, but I heard the door of the master bedroom opening, the bedroom in which Hélie would be sleeping, and I heard it close. I thought that perhaps, immediately after that, I would hear the doctor's footsteps, he having left Claudia in her room in order to leave the house, now that his medical mission had been fulfilled. But that isn't what happened, the penultimate thing I heard that night was the closing of the master bedroom door, which the night doctor had also entered, very quietly and holding a syringe in his left hand.

With great care (I took off my shoes), I walked down the corridor to my room. I undressed, got into bed and finished reading the newspaper. Before turning out the light, I waited a few seconds and it was in those brief seconds of waiting that I at last heard the front door and Claudia's voice saying goodbye to the doctor in Spanish: "See you in a fortnight then. Goodnight, and thanks." The truth is that I still felt like speaking a little more of my own language on that night on which I had twice missed the opportunity of doing so with my compatriot the doctor.

I was going back to Madrid the following morning. Before leaving, I had time to ask Claudia how she was, and she said she was fine, that the pains had gone. Hélie, on the other hand, was indisposed after the various excesses of the previous night and said he was sorry not to be able to say goodbye to me himself.

I spoke to him on the phone after that (that is, he picked up the phone on one occasion when I called Claudia from Madrid in the months that followed), but the last time I saw him was when I left his apartment that night, after the supper for seven, to walk the Italian friend, whose name I cannot remember, back to her apartment. Precisely because I cannot remember her name, I do not know if the next time I go to Paris, I will dare to ask Claudia how she is, because now that Hélie is dead, I wouldn't want to run the risk of finding out that perhaps she too has become a widow since my departure.

THE ITALIAN LEGACY

Lo stesso

I HAVE TWO Italian women friends, who both live in Paris. Until a couple of years ago, they had never met, they had never seen each other, I introduced them one summer, I was the link and I'm afraid to say I still am, although they have not seen each other since. From the time that they met, or rather, saw each other and became aware that I knew both of them, their lives have changed far too rapidly and not so much in parallel as consecutively. I don't know if I should stop seeing the one in order to liberate the other, or change the nature of my relationship with the other in order to have the first one disappear from her life. I don't know what to do, I don't know if I should say anything.

Initially, they had nothing in common, apart from a considerable mutual interest in books and, therefore, their respective libraries, each created with patience, devotion and care. The friend I had known longest, Giulia, was an amateur: the daughter of a former ambassador, a *misino* (i.e a neo-fascist), she was married and had two children, she rented out a few apartments that she owned in Rome, she lived off the rent and did not work, she could devote almost all her time to her passion, reading, and her social life was limited to inviting writers to her house in a pale emulation of French *salonnières* of the eighteenth century such as Madame du Deffand (what more can one expect nowadays?). My more recent friend, Silvia, on the other hand, was a professional: she edited a series for a publisher, she was slightly younger, single, with no assets, and she scraped a living writing for Italian newspapers – interviews and articles on books; she didn't invite anyone to her house, but instead went out and met writers in cafés, in cinemas, sometimes for supper. As for me, despite being a foreigner to them and a foreigner in the city, Silvia would meet me somewhere and Giulia would invite me home. When Giulia invited me home, her husband used to go out for a few hours because he hated all things Spanish. He was an older man, twenty years older than his wife, and a writer himself (albeit of treatises on engineering), in possession of a precarious fortune of which Giulia made only moderate use. Then one summer, her husband had to go away for a considerable period, for professional reasons. From the kitchen window, Giulia began to notice a young man who lived a few floors below. She always saw him sitting down, with his glasses on, but without his shirt, apparently studying. Later, they passed on the stairs, and by the time her husband returned they had become lovers, they would leave letters in each other's mail boxes, with no return address on the back. Only a month later, her husband asked for a divorce and left the apartment. The neighbour came and went up and down the stairs.

It was then that my other friend, Silvia, announced to me that she was getting married. One of those older writers with whom she used to go out to the café or to the cinema had become so much a part of her life that she couldn't do without him. He was twenty years older than her, very intelligent (she said), he wrote treatises on Islam, he had something of a reputation and a personal fortune inherited from his first wife, who had died ten years before. The only thing that alerted me then was the fact that, as Silvia laughingly told me, he hated all things Spanish, and so, when I visited Paris, she would perhaps have to continue meeting me in cafés and cinemas. It occurred to me that his hatred might have Moorish roots.

Meanwhile, Giulia, the first friend, devoted herself to leading the kind of life with the false student (his glasses made him look younger, he was a man of thirty-something, the same age as her, and had a good job as a psychologist with a big multinational) which, given his age and character, her husband had never wanted or been able to lead: not only in summer, like a large part of the world's population, but during every vacation period, they set off on complicated journeys to far-away places: in the space of nine months they visited Bali, Malaysia and, finally, Thailand. It was in Thailand that, for no known reason, the psychologist or false student fell ill, and his case provoked such interest amongst the hospital doctors that even the Queen's doctor dropped in to have a look at him. No one knew what he had, but after fifteen anxious days, he recovered and was able to return to Paris.

It was more or less then, that, unexpectedly (only months, not years, had passed since her marriage), Silvia, during a time when her Islamic husband was immobilized due to a fall down the stairs in their new conjugal home (so many houses in Paris still do not have a lift), she happened to meet in a cinema (to which this time she went alone) a young man of her own age for whom, after a few more weeks of cinemas and cafés and marital immobility, she had conceived such a passion that she had no option but to propose a quickie divorce and to acknowledge her mistake (that is, her impatience or her weakness or her submission to habit, or her resignation). The young man was rather richer than the old writer: he was deputy director of a canning factory for mussels and tuna and was constantly visiting far-off countries in order to make acquisitions or to carry out murky deals. Silvia went with him to China and then Korea and later to Vietnam. It was in this latter country that, for no known reason, the deputy director of the canning factory fell gravely ill and had to postpone his many deals during the two unplanned-for weeks that it took him to recover.

I had never spoken to Giulia about Silvia or to Silvia about Giulia, because neither of them is interested in other people's lives and it seems impolite to entrust to other ears things which, in principle, were intended only for mine. Now, however, I have my doubts, because this summer, I visited Giulia in Paris and her situation has taken a rather worrying turn: ever since, three months ago, she and the false student or psychologist decided to live in the same apartment, he has turned out to be a very nasty piece of work indeed: he hates books now and has forced Giulia to get rid of her library; he beats her, he's violent; and recently, while she was pretending to be asleep, she has twice seen him standing at the foot of the bed stroking a razor (once, she says, he was sharpening it on a strap like an old-fashioned barber). Giulia trusts that it will be a passing phase, a consequence of the enigmatic illness contracted in Thailand or some upset caused by the unbearable heat of this never-ending summer. I hope so, but given that Silvia and her canner are thinking of moving in together, perhaps I should speak to her now, even if only so that she can save her library and try to persuade her man to change to an electric razor.

THE HONEYMOON

M Y WIFE HAD suddenly felt ill and we had rushed back
to our hotel room, where she had lain down, shivering
and feeling slightly nauseous and feverish. We didn't want to
call a doctor immediately in case it passed off of its own accord
and because we were on our honeymoon, and on honeymoon
you really don't want the interference of a stranger, even if it's
for a medical examination. It was probably a minor stomach
upset, colic or something. We were in Seville, in a hotel sheltered
from the traffic by an esplanade that separated it from the street.
While my wife was sleeping (she seemed to fall asleep as soon as
I had undressed her and covered her up), I decided to keep
quiet, and the best way to do that and not be tempted to make
any noise or to talk to her out of sheer boredom was to go over
to the balcony and watch the people passing by, the people of
Seville, how they walked and how they dressed, how they talked,
even though, given the relative distance of the street and the
traffic, you could hear only a murmur. I looked without seeing,
like someone who arrives at a party from which he knows the
only person who really interests him will be absent, having
stayed at home with her husband. That one person was with me,

behind me, watched over by her husband. I was looking outside, but thinking about what was happening inside, however, I did suddenly pick out one person, and I picked her out because unlike the other people, who walked by and then disappeared, that person remained motionless in one place. It was a woman who, from a distance, looked about thirty, and was wearing an almost sleeveless blue blouse, a white skirt and white high heels. She was waiting for someone, her attitude unmistakably that of someone waiting, because every now and then she would take two or three steps to the right or the left, and on the last step she would drag the stiletto heel of one foot or the other, a gesture of suppressed impatience. On her arm she carried a large handbag, like the bags that mothers, my mother, carried when I was a child, a large black handbag carried on the arm, not slung over the shoulder the way women wear them now. She had strong legs that dug solidly into the pavement each time she returned to the spot where she had chosen to wait after that minimal movement to either side of two or three steps, dragging her heel on the final step. Her legs were so strong that they cancelled out or assimilated her high heels, it was her legs that dug into the pavement, like a knife into wet wood. Sometimes she would bend one leg in order to look behind and smooth her skirt, as if she feared that some crease might be spoiling the line of her skirt at the rear or perhaps she was simply adjusting the elastic of a recalcitrant pair of knickers through the fabric covering them.

It was growing dark, and the gradually fading light made her seem to me ever more solitary, more isolated and more condemned to wait in vain. Her date would not arrive. She was standing in the middle of the pavement, she did not lean against the wall as those who wait usually do, so as not to get in the way of those passers-by who are not waiting, which is why she had trouble avoiding them, one man said something to her and she responded angrily and threatened him with her voluminous bag.

Suddenly she looked up, at the third floor where I was standing on the balcony, and she seemed to fix her eyes on me for the first time. She peered at me, as if she were short-sighted or were looking through grubby contact lenses, she screwed up her eyes a little to see better, it was, it seemed, me she was looking at. But I knew no one in Seville, more than that, it was the first time I had ever been to Seville, on my honeymoon, with my brand-new wife lying ill on the bed behind me, I just hoped it was nothing serious. I heard a murmur coming from the bed, but I didn't turn round because it was a moan made in her sleep, one quickly learns to distinguish the sounds the person one sleeps with makes in their sleep. The woman had taken a few more steps, this time in my direction, she was crossing the street, dodging the cars, not bothering to look for traffic lights, as if she wanted to get closer quickly in order to find out, to get a better view of me on my balcony. She walked slowly, however, and with difficulty, as if she were unaccustomed to wearing high heels or as if her striking legs weren't used to them, or as if her handbag threw her off balance or as if she were dizzy. She walked rather in the way that my wife had walked after being taken ill, when she came into the room, I had helped her to undress and put her to bed, I had covered her up. The woman had just crossed the street, now she was closer but still some way off, separated from the hotel by the ample esplanade that set it back from the traffic. She continued looking up at me or at where I was, at the building in which I was staying. And then she made a gesture with her arm, a gesture that neither greeted nor beckoned, I mean it wasn't the way one would beckon to a stranger, it was a gesture of appropriation and recognition, as if I were the person she had been waiting for and as if her date was with me. It was as if with that gesture of her arm, finished off by a swift flourish of the fingers, she wanted to grab hold of me and say: "Come here," or "You're mine". At the same time she shouted something that I couldn't hear and from the movement of her lips I understood only the first word and that word was "Hey!" uttered with great indignation as was the rest of the phrase that failed to reach my ears. She continued to advance, she smoothed the rear of her skirt more earnestly now because it seemed that the person who would judge her appearance was there before her, the person she was waiting for could now appreciate the way her skirt fell. And then I did hear what she was saying: "Hey, what are you doing up there?" The shout was very audible now, and I could see the woman better. Perhaps she was older than thirty, she still had her eyes screwed up, but they seemed light in colour to me, grey or hazel, and she had full lips, a rather broad nose, her nostrils flaring vehemently, out of anger, she must have spent a long time waiting, far longer than the time that had elapsed since I had picked her out. She stumbled as she walked, she tripped and fell to the ground, instantly dirtying her white skirt and losing one of her shoes. She struggled to her feet, as if she feared getting her foot dirty too, now that her date had arrived, now that she needed to have clean feet just in case the man she had arranged to meet should see them. She managed to get her shoe back on without putting her foot on the ground, she brushed down her skirt and shouted: "What are you doing up there! Why didn't you tell me you'd already gone up? I've been waiting for you here for an hour!" And as she said that, she repeated the same grasping gesture, a bare arm beating the air and the quick flourish of fingers that accompanied it. It was as if she were saying: "You're mine" or "I'll kill you," as if with that gesture she could grab me and drag me towards her, like a claw. This time she shouted something and she was so close I was afraid she might wake my wife.

"What's wrong?" said my wife feebly.

I turned round, she was sitting up in bed, with frightened eyes, the eyes of a sick person who wakes and cannot see anything and doesn't yet know where she is or why she feels so confused. The light was off. At that moment, she was a sick woman.

"It's nothing, go back to sleep," I said.

But I didn't walk over to her to stroke her hair or calm her down, as I would have done in any other circumstances, because I couldn't leave the balcony, or even take my eyes off that woman who was convinced she had arranged to meet me. Now she could see me clearly, and I was obviously the person with whom she had made an important date, the person who had caused her to suffer by making her wait and who had offended her with my prolonged absence. "Didn't you notice I'd been waiting for you here for an hour? Why didn't you say something?" she was yelling furiously now, standing outside my hotel, beneath my balcony. "Do you hear me, I'm going to kill you!" she shouted. And again she made the gesture with her arm and her fingers, the grasping gesture.

"What on earth's going on?" asked my wife again, lying dazed on the bed.

At that moment, I stepped back and pulled the balcony shutters to, but not before seeing that the woman in the street, with her enormous, old-fashioned handbag and her stiletto heels and her strong legs and her stumbling walk, was disappearing from my field of vision because she was entering the hotel, ready to come up and find me and meet me. I felt empty inside when I thought about what I could possibly say to my sick wife to explain the interruption that was about to take place. We were on our honeymoon and on honeymoon you really don't want the interference of a stranger, although I was not, I think, a stranger to the person now coming up the stairs. I felt empty inside and I closed the balcony shutters. I prepared myself to open the door.

BROKEN BINOCULARS

For Mercedes López-Ballesteros,
in San Sebastián

O N PALM SUNDAY, almost all my friends had left Madrid, and so I went to spend the afternoon at the races. In the second race, which was not particularly interesting, a man to my left inadvertently jolted my elbow as he abruptly raised his binoculars to his eyes in order to get a better view of the final straight. I was already looking, I already had my binoculars before my eyes, and the sudden blow made me drop them (I always forget to hang them round my neck, and that's how I pay for it or how I paid on that day, because one of the lenses cracked, the binoculars hit the steps, they didn't bounce, they just lay there on the ground, still and broken). The man crouched down before I could pick them up, he was the one who first noticed the damage, apologizing as he did so.

"Sorry," he said. And then: "Oh no, what bad luck, they're broken."

I saw him crouched at my feet and the first thing I noticed was that he was wearing cufflinks, a rare sight nowadays, only the very vulgar or the very ancient dare wear them. The second thing I noticed was that he had a gun in a holster strapped to his right side (he must have been left-handed), as he bent down his jacket gaped open at the back and I saw the butt of the gun. Now that's an even rarer sight, he must be a policeman, I thought. Then, as he got up, I realized that he was a very tall man, a whole head taller than me; he must have been about thirty and he had side-burns, straight but much too long, another old-fashioned touch, I wouldn't have noticed them fifteen or even a hundred years ago. Perhaps he wore them to frame and add volume to his head, which was long and rather small, he looked like a matchstick.

"I'll pay for any repairs," he said, embarrassed. "Here, I'll lend you mine for the moment. It's only the second race."

The second race had, in fact, finished. We didn't know who had won, so I didn't dare tear up my betting slips, which I held in my hand as we all do, only to tear them up and immediately throw them to the ground if we've lost, and thus instantly forget our mistaken forecast. At that moment, I was also holding my broken binoculars (I'd bought them on a plane not long before, in mid-flight) as well as the other man's undamaged ones, he had handed them to me at the same time as he had announced that they were mine to borrow, I had taken them mechanically so that they too did not crash onto the steps. When he saw that I had my hands full, he relieved me of the betting slips and put them in the breast pocket of my jacket and gave it a little pat, as if to say that they were now in safekeeping.

"But if you give me yours, what are you going to do?" I said.

"We can share them, if you don't mind us watching the races together," he said. "Are you on your own?"

"Yes, I am."

"The only thing is," the man added, "we'd have to watch all the races from here. I'm on surveillance duty, and this is my post today. I can't move from here."

"Are you a policeman?"

"Bloody hell, no, I'd starve. I know a few though. Besides,

do you think I could dress the way I do if I was a policeman?
Look at me."

And as he said that, the man stretched out his arms and took a
step back, his hands outspread as if he were a magician. The fact
is that (to my taste) he was extremely badly, albeit expensively,
dressed: a double-breasted suit (but with the jacket open, as I
said) in an unlikely greenish-grey colour, undoubtedly difficult
to find; the shirt, which seemed overly starched for the times, was,
I fear, wine, not an ugly colour in itself, but inappropriate in such
a tall man; his tie was an incomprehensible swarm (birds, insects,
repellent Mirós, cats' eyes), in which the predominant colour was
yellow; the oddest thing were his shoes: they weren't lace-ups or
moccasins, they were like children's ankle-high bootees, he must
have thought them very modern, and the rest he would imagine
was semi-classic. His cufflinks weren't too bad, possibly by Durán,
very shiny and in the shape of a leaf. He was not a discreet man,
nor original, he had simply never been taught how to coordinate
his clothes.

"I see," I said, not knowing what to say. "So what have you
got to watch?"

"I'm a bodyguard," he said.

"Oh, and who are you guarding?"

The man took the binoculars that he had just lent me and
peered through them at the grandstand which was a short
distance away (you didn't really need magnifying lenses to see
it). He handed them back to me. He seemed relieved.

"He hasn't arrived yet, there's still time. If he does come, he
won't get here until the fourth race, to say hello to his friends.
Like everyone else, he's only really interested in the fifth race, and
he can't waste a moment, I mean, you probably came early just
to pass the time. He, on the other hand, will be doing deals over
the phone or taking a nap so as to have a clear head. I came early,

just to see how things are going this afternoon, to check that things aren't getting heavy here and to take any necessary steps."

"Heavy? What do you mean? What could possibly happen here?"

"Probably nothing, but someone always has to go on ahead. And someone else stays behind with him, of course. I'm usually the one who goes on ahead. For example, if we're going to a restaurant or a casino, or we stop to have a beer at a roadside bar, I always go in first to see the way the land lies. You never know when you go into a public place, two guys might be beating the hell out of each other at that very moment. It doesn't happen very often, but you never know, a waiter might have spilled some wine, and an awkward customer might be giving him a hard time. I wouldn't want my boss to see that or have him mixed up in a mess like that. Before you know it, bottles are flying. During the day a lot more bottles go flying about in Madrid than you might imagine, knives come out, people hit each other, people can be very thin-skinned. And if, in the middle of all this, someone with a bit of money turns up, then everyone stops and thinks: 'Let the rich man pay.' The ones doing the fighting are quite capable of coming to some instant agreement and laying into the man with the dosh: 'To hell with the rich.' You have to keep a very sharp eye out."

The man raised a finger to his eye.

"Really?" I said. "Is your boss that rich, then? Is it so obvious?"

"It's written all over his face, he's got the face of a rich man. Even if he didn't shave for three days and dressed like a beggar, you could tell from his face he was rich. I wish I had that face. Whenever we go into an expensive shop, I go first, as usual. And despite the fact that I'm well dressed, as soon as the assistants see me they pull a face or ignore me, pretend they haven't seen me, they start serving other customers who they hadn't taken a blind bit of notice of before or they start rummaging around in drawers as if they were stocktaking. I don't say a word, I just check that everything's all right and then I go back to the door to open it for the boss and let him in. And as soon as they see his face, the assistants abandon their other customers and the drawers they were rummaging in to come and serve him, all smiles."

"Isn't it just that they recognize your boss because he's famous, if he's as rich as you say he is?"

"Possibly," said the bodyguard, as if that hadn't occurred to him. "He is getting quite well known. He's in banking, you know. I won't tell you who with, but he is. But listen, why don't we go down to the paddock for a bit, it'll be time to start betting on the third race soon."

So we did and, on the way, we finally tore up our tickets and threw them to the ground, huh, when we saw that we had lost. I passed a philosopher who's there every Sunday, as well as Admiral Admira (with his predestined and incomplete surname) and his lovely and undeserved wife, who both nodded to me without saying a word, as if they were embarrassed to see me in the company of that rather gigantic individual, I only came up to his shoulder. I was now wearing his binoculars round my neck and carrying my own broken pair, mine are small and powerful, his were enormous and very heavy, the strap cut into my neck, but I couldn't run the risk of dropping them as well. While we were watching the horses walking round the paddock, I sensed that the bodyguard was about to ask me what I did, and since I didn't feel like talking about myself, I got in first and said:

"What do you think of number fourteen?"

"He looks good," he said, which is what those who know nothing about horses always say. "I think I might bet on him."

"I don't think I will, he looks a bit highly-strung to me. He might even get stuck at the starting gate."

"Really, do you think so?"

"Having a rich man's face counts for nothing here."

The man burst out laughing. It was a spontaneous laugh, without the slightest forethought, the laugh of an unpolished man, the laugh of a man who does not stop to worry about whether or not it is appropriate to laugh. What I'd said wasn't that funny. Then, without asking my permission, he grabbed his binoculars and looked quickly through them at the grandstand, which you couldn't actually see from the paddock. It hurt my neck, the man pulled too hard on the strap.

"So, has he arrived yet?" I said.

"No, luckily he hasn't," he said, going by instinct, I assume.

"Does he give you a lot of work? I mean, do you often have to intervene, intervene seriously I mean, when it's dangerous."

"Not as much as I'd like, really, it's very stressful this job, but at the same time, very inactive, you have to be permanently on the alert, you have to anticipate trouble, on a couple of occasions I've grabbed hold of really distinguished people who were just going up to my boss to say hello. I've pinned their hands behind their backs and overpowered them, for no reason at all, they've even been on the receiving end of a few expert blows. I got hauled over the coals for it too. So you have to be very careful and not anticipate too much. You have to guess people's intentions, that's what you have to do. Not that anything much ever happens, and it's difficult to stay alert if you have the feeling that it's not really necessary."

"I suppose you tend to lower your guard a bit."

"No, I don't, but I have a really hard time making sure that I don't. My colleague, the one who stays with him while I go on ahead, I notice that he lowers his guard much more. I tell him off about it sometimes. He plays portable video games while he's waiting, he's a bit of an addict. And you just can't do that, you see."

"Yes, I see. And how does the boss treat you both?"

"Well, for him we're invisible, he doesn't not do anything just because we're there. I've seen him get up to some really disgusting things."

"What sort of disgusting things?"

The bodyguard took my arm and led me over to the betting booths. I felt suddenly embarrassed to be walking along like that with such a tall man. His way of taking my arm was protective, perhaps he didn't know how to make contact with people in any other way: he was always the protector. He seemed to hesitate for a moment. Then he said:

"Well, with women, in the car, for example. In fact, he's a bit of a dirty old man, got a dirty mind, you know?" He tapped his forehead. "Listen, you're not a journalist, are you?"

"No, not at all."

"Good."

I bet on number eight and he bet on number fourteen, he was a stubborn man, or else superstitious, and we went back to the stands. We sat down, waiting for the third race to begin.

"What shall we do about the binoculars?"

"What if I watch the start and you watch the finish?" he said. "After all, it was my fault."

He again took the binoculars from me without first removing them from around my neck, but now we were sitting very close together and there was no need for him to pull on the strap. He looked at the grandstand for a second and then replaced the binoculars on my knees. I looked at his bootees, they seemed so incongruous, they made his very large feet look childish. He got excited during the race, shouting: "Go on, *Narnia*, move it!" at number fourteen which did not get stuck at the gate, but nevertheless got off to a bad start and only came in fourth. My number eight was in second place, so we both tore up our slips with an appropriately embittered look on our faces: ah, to hell with it.

Suddenly, I noticed that he looked depressed, it couldn't be because of the bet.

"Are you all right?" I asked.

He didn't answer at once. He was looking at the floor, at his torn-up tickets, he had his broad chest thrown forward, his head almost between his spread legs, as if he felt sick and was taking precautions in case he had to throw up, so as not to stain his trousers.

"No," he said at last. "It's just that that was the third race, my boss will be about to arrive with my colleague, if they arrive that is. And if they arrive, then it'll be up to me."

"I suppose you have to stay here and keep watch."

"Yes, I do. Do you mind keeping me company? Well, if you want to go down to the paddock and place a bet, you go ahead and then come back for the race. I'll stay here with the binoculars, just in case anything should happen."

"I'll just nip down and place my bet. I don't need to see the horses."

He gave me ten thousand pesetas for the first two past the post, another five thousand for a winner, I went down to place my bets, I was only gone a matter of moments, the queue hadn't started yet. When I got back to the stand, the bodyguard was still sitting with his head down, he didn't seem particularly alert. He was stroking his sideburns, absorbed in thought.

"Has he arrived yet?" I asked, just to say something.

"No, not yet," he replied raising first his eyes and then the binoculars to the grandstand. It had become an almost mechanical gesture. "I might not have to do it after all."

The man still seemed depressed, he had suddenly lost all his bonhomie, as if a cloud were hanging over him. He no longer chatted to me or paid me any attention. I felt tempted to say that I would prefer to see that race by the track, where I could manage perfectly well without binoculars, and leave him to himself. But I feared for his job. He was sunk in thought, and not at all vigilant, just when he needed to be.

"Are you sure you're all right?" I said, and then, more than anything in order to remind him of the imminence of his task. "If you're not feeling well, do you want me to watch for you? If you tell me who your boss is . . ."

"There's nothing to watch," he replied. "I know what's going to happen this afternoon. It may have happened already."

"What?"

"Look, you don't get fond of someone who pays you to protect them. Like I said, my boss doesn't even know I exist, he barely knows my name, I've been as invisible as air to him for the last two years, and from time to time he's bawled me out because I was over-zealous. He gives orders and I carry them out, he tells me when and where he wants me and I go there, at the time and place indicated, that's all. I take care that nothing happens to him, but I don't feel fond of him. On more than one occasion, I've even thought of attacking him myself just to ease the tension and make myself feel necessary, to create the danger myself. Nothing serious, just rough him up a bit in the garage, do a bit of play-acting, hide somewhere and pass myself off as a mugger in my spare time. Give him a fright. I never imagined that the day would come when we'd have to knock him off for real."

"Knock him off? And who's we?"

"My colleague and me. Well, either him or me. He might have managed to do it already; I hope so. If he has, the boss won't appear for this race either, he won't even have left the house and he'll be lying on the carpet, or stuffed in the boot of the car. But if he does come, you see, it will mean that my colleague didn't manage to do it, and then I'll have to, on the way back from the race course, in the car itself, while my colleague does the driving. With a length of rope, or a single shot once we're off the road. I really hope they don't come, I don't much like him, but the idea of having to kill him myself . . . It makes me feel ill."

I thought he was joking, but until that moment he hadn't seemed like a man much given to jokes, he'd seemed almost incapable of them, that's why – I thought fleetingly – he had laughed so much when I made that one rather unfunny remark. People who don't know how to make jokes are so surprised and grateful when others do.

"I'm not sure I understand," I said.

He kept rubbing furiously at his sideburns. He looked at me out of the corner of his eye and remained staring at me like that.

"Of course you do, I explained it perfectly clearly. Like I said, I don't much like him, but I'd be relieved if they didn't come, if my colleague had already done it."

"Why are you doing it?"

"It's a long story. For money, well, not just that, sometimes you have no option, sometimes you have to do things that disgust you, but you have to do them all the same, because it would be worse not to, hasn't that ever happened to you?"

"Yes, it has," I said, "but never anything so drastic." I glanced at the grandstand, a pointless gesture on my part. "If this is all true, why are you telling me?"

"It really doesn't make any difference. You're not going to tell anyone else, even if you read about it in the paper tomorrow. Nobody likes getting involved in bother; if you go and tell somebody, you'll get nothing but complications and a lot of trouble. And threats too probably. No one tells anyone anything unless they're going to benefit in some way. Not even God helps the police, everyone thinks, oh, let them get on with it. And no one says anything. You'll do the same. I don't feel like having any secrets today."

I picked up the binoculars and looked again at the grand-stand, with the lenses on full magnification. It was almost empty, everyone must have gone to the bar or to the paddock, it was still some minutes before the race was due to start. That gesture was all the more useless, because I didn't even know his boss, although, if I saw him, I might guess who he was by his rich man's face.

"Is he there?" he asked me fearfully, looking at the track.

"I don't think so, there's hardly anyone. You look."

"No, I prefer to wait. When the race is about to start, when they all come in. Will you tell me?"

"Yes, I'll tell you."

We fell silent. I glanced again at his boots (his feet were very close together now) and he was staring at the cufflinks on his shirt, his wine shirt, his cufflinks in the form of tobacco leaves. Suddenly I found myself hoping that a man was dead, that his boss was already dead. I found myself preferring that option, so that he wouldn't have to kill him. We started to notice the stand filling up, people were pressing in on us, we had to get to our feet to make room.

"You have the binoculars," I said, "we agreed that you would watch the start of the race." And I handed them to him.

The bodyguard took them and raised them brusquely to his eyes, with the same gesture that had rendered mine unusable. I saw him focus them on the starting boxes and then, when the horses were under orders, he turned the binoculars towards the grandstand for a few seconds. I heard him counting:

"One, two, three, four, five, six, seven, eight, nine, ten. He hasn't come," he said.

"They're off," I said.

He looked again at the track and when the horses were taking the first bend, I heard him shouting:

"Go on, *Charon*, go on! Come on, *Charon*, come on!"

Despite his excitement and his joy, he was still clearheaded enough to pass me the binoculars when the horses were reaching the final bend. He was a considerate man, he kept his promise to let me watch the finish. I raised the binoculars to my eyes and I saw that *Charon* was winning by half a length over *Heart So White* in second place: the two horses that my companion had bet on that afternoon to win and to come second. I, on the other hand, would have to tear up my tickets once more and throw them to the ground.

I lowered the binoculars and I was surprised not to hear him shouting and happy.

"You won," I said.

But he obviously hadn't followed the last part of the race, he obviously didn't know. He was staring at the grandstand with his own eyes, without the help of binoculars. He was very still. He turned to me without looking at me, as if I were a stranger. I was a stranger. He buttoned up his jacket. His face had grown dark again, almost contorted.

"There they are, they've arrived. They've arrived for the fifth race," he said. "I'm sorry, I must go and join them, he'll want to give me instructions."

He said nothing more, not even goodbye. He had pushed his way through the crowds in a matter of moments and I watched him from behind, a giant figure moving off towards the grandstand. As he walked, he patted his jacket on his right side, the gun in its holster. He had left his binoculars with me. I tore up my tickets but not his winning tickets. I put them in my pocket, he was unlikely to want to claim them, I thought.

shame the background isn't finished," and he examined it closely, despite the fact that the light wasn't good. The same light lit the bed much better. "No one will have visited that bed in ten years," he thought, "possibly more." Custardoy is always thinking about the contents of beds.

That night there was a storm and, from his room on the second floor, Custardoy heard the lame dog barking. He remembered the rabbit gin, that wouldn't be the reason this time, though, but the thunder. He went over to the window to see if the dog was anywhere in sight, and he saw it there, by the rain-drenched sea – pellets falling on a shaken length of cloth – standing there like a tripod and barking at the zigzag lightning, as if he were waiting for each flash. "Perhaps there was a storm on the night when he got caught in the trap," Custardoy thought, "and now he's no longer afraid of the lightning." He had just had that thought when he saw the little servant girl come running up in her nightdress, she was carrying a lead in her hand with which to secure the dog and drag him away. He saw her struggling, her body clearly outlined beneath her drenched clothes, and he heard an anguished voice immediately beneath his own window: "You're going to get killed, you're going to get killed!" said the voice. "Nobody sleeps in this house," he thought. "Apart, perhaps, from Cámara." He noiselessly opened the window and leaned out a little, not wanting to be seen. He felt the heavy rain on the back of his neck and what he saw from above was an opened black umbrella, Señora Vallabriga waiting anxiously for the return of those two unfinished figures, it was her voice, hers the bare arm that, from time to time, he could see reaching out from beneath the umbrella, as if she wanted to attract or grab both the dog and the little girl, struggling together, the dog with the missing leg could hardly run away or escape, it kept barking at the lightning that lit up its eyes, the reluctant eyes of a languid boyfriend, and the girl's body that seemed more adult than it did when clothed – her body suddenly finished and complete. Custardoy wondered who it was that the aunt feared was going to be killed, and he soon found out, when the girl finally reached the door, dragging the dog, and the three of them disappeared, first beneath the umbrella like a cupola and then into the house. He closed the window and, from within, he heard just two more sentences, both spoken by the aunt, the girl must have been rendered speechless: "Look at that little mutt," she said. And then: "Into bed this minute, my girl, and take that off." Custardoy heard weary footsteps coming up to his floor and then, when he was once more lying down in bed and when silence had fallen after the final noise of one door closing – just one door – he wondered if perhaps he had been wrong about the bed that guarded the Goya and that no one would visit. He didn't wonder too long, but he decided that the following morning he would commit an act of betrayal: the report he had to give to Cámara about the possibilities of a forgery would say that it wasn't worth forging a copy. The young girl who would inherit the Goya had certainly earned it. He would tell Cámara: "Forget it."

Note: The character of the servant girl and the implied lesbianism in this mini-story came about because the five obligatory elements imposed by the commission (a veritable Chinese torture) immediately made me think of *Rebecca* – in either Alfred Hitchcock's or Daphne du Maurier's version.

FLESH SUNDAY

WE WERE STAYING in the Hotel de Londres and, during our first twenty-four hours in the city we hadn't left our room, we had merely been out onto the terrace to look at La Concha beach, far too crowded for the spectacle to be a pleasant one. An indistinguishable mass is never a pleasing sight, and it was impossible there to fix on anyone, even with binoculars, an excess of bare flesh has a distinctly levelling effect. We had taken the binoculars with us just in case, one Sunday, we went to Lasarte, to the races, there's not much to do in San Sebastián on a Sunday in August, we would be there for three weeks on our holidays, four Sundays but only three weeks, because that second day of our stay was a Sunday and we would be leaving on a Monday.

I spent more time out on the terrace than did my wife, Luisa, always with my binoculars in my hand, or rather, hanging round my neck so that they didn't slip from my grasp and fall from the terrace to shatter on the ground below. I tried to focus on someone on the beach, to pick someone out, but there were too many people to be able to remain faithful to anyone in particular, I panned across the beach with the binoculars, I saw hundreds of children, dozens of fat men, scores of girls (none of them topless, that's still fairly rare in San Sebastián), young flesh, mature flesh and old flesh, children's flesh which is not yet flesh and mother's flesh which is somehow more fleshly for having already reproduced itself. I soon grew tired of looking and went back to the bed where Luisa was lying down, I kissed her a few times, then returned to the terrace, and again peered through the binoculars. Perhaps I was bored, which is why I felt slightly envious when I saw that two rooms down to my right there was a man, also armed with binoculars, who had them trained on one particular spot, lowering them only from time to time and not moving them at all when he was looking through them: he held them up high, motionless, for a couple of minutes, then he would rest his arm and, shortly afterwards, he would raise it again, always in the same position, he didn't change the direction of his gaze one inch. He wasn't leaning out, though, he was watching from inside his room, and so I could only see one hairy arm, now where exactly was he looking, I wondered enviously, I wanted to fix my gaze on something too, it's only when you rest your gaze on something that you really relax and become interested in what you're looking at, I merely made random sweeps, just flesh and yet more indistinguishable flesh, if, when we finally left the room, Luisa and I went down to the beach (we were killing time until it got a bit emptier, possibly around lunchtime), we would form part of that conglomeration of distant, identical flesh, our recognizable bodies would be lost in the uniformity created by sand and water and swimming costumes, especially by swimming costumes. And that man to my right would not notice us, no one looking down from above – as he and I were doing – would notice us once we formed part of that disagreeable spectacle. Perhaps that's why, in order not to be seen, in order not to be focused on or marked out, holiday-makers like to take off a few clothes and mingle with other half-naked people amidst the sand and the sea.

I tried to work out where that man, my neighbour, was looking, and I managed to fix on a space that was not small enough for me to rest my gaze on entirely and take an interest in whatever it was that was interesting, but at least in that way, by imitating or trying to guess the direction of his gaze, I could discount most of everything else that lay before me, an entire beach.

"What are you looking at?" my wife asked from the bed. It was very hot and she had placed a wet towel on her forehead, it almost covered her eyes, which were not in the least interested in looking at anything.

"I don't know yet," I said without turning round. "I'm trying to see what another man here beside me on a neighbouring balcony is looking at."

"Why? What does it matter to you? Don't be so nosy."

It didn't matter to me, in fact, but in summer wasting time is what you try hardest to do, if not, you don't really feel that it's summer, which is supposed to be slow and purposeless.

According to my calculations and observations, the man to my right had to be looking at one of four people, all fairly close together and lined up in the back row, far from the water's edge. To the right of these people was a small empty space, to their left as well, which was what made me think that he was looking at one of those four. The first person (from left to right, as they say in photo captions) had her face turned to me or us, for she was sunbathing lying on her back: a youngish woman, she was reading a newspaper, she had the top part of her bikini undone, but hadn't removed it entirely (that's still rather frowned upon in San Sebastián). The second person was sitting down, she was older, plumper, wearing a one-piece bathing suit and a straw hat, she was smearing suncream on herself: she must be a mother, but her children were nowhere to be seen, perhaps they were playing by the sea. The third person was a man, possibly her husband or her brother, he was thinner, he was pretending to shiver as he stood on his towel, as if he had just emerged from the sea (he must have been pretending to shiver because the sea would certainly not be cold). The fourth person was the easiest to make out because he was wearing clothes, at least his top half was covered: he was an older man (the hair at the nape of his neck was grey) sitting with his back to us, erect, as if he, in turn, were watching or surveying someone on the shore or some rows ahead, the beach his theatre. I fixed my gaze on him: he was evidently alone, he had nothing to do with the man to his left, the man who was pretending to shiver. He was wearing a short-sleeved, green T-shirt, you couldn't see if he had swimming trunks on or trousers, if he was fully dressed, most inappropriate on a beach, if he was, that would certainly attract attention. He was scratching his back, scratching his waist, he had a lot of fat around his waist, it must have weighed on him, he was one of those men who have great difficulty getting to their feet, to do so they have to throw their arms forward, with their fingers outstretched as if someone were pulling them. He was scratching his back, almost as if he were pointing to it. I didn't have time to find out if he would get to his feet like that, with difficulty, nor if he was wearing trousers or swimming trunks, but I did find out that he was the man my neighbour was looking at, because suddenly, with my binoculars fixed at last on his thick waist and his broad back, I saw him collapse, fall forwards in a sitting position, the way puppets fall when the hand holding them lets go of the strings. I had heard a brief, muffled noise, and I just had time to see that what was disappearing from the balcony to my right was not the arm of my neighbour with the binoculars, but his arm and the barrel of a gun. I don't think anyone realized what had happened, although the man who had been shivering abruptly stopped, no longer cold.

WHEN I WAS MORTAL

I OFTEN USED to pretend I believed in ghosts, and I did so blithely, but now that I am myself a ghost, I understand why, traditionally, they are depicted as mournful creatures who stubbornly return to the places they knew when they were mortal. For they do return. Very rarely are they or we noticed, the houses we lived in have changed and the people who live in them do not even know of our past existence, they cannot even imagine it: like children, these men and women believe that the world began with their birth, and they never wonder if, on the ground they tread, others once trod with lighter steps or with fateful footfalls, if between the walls that shelter them others heard whispers or laughter, or if someone once read a letter out loud, or strangled the person he most loved. It's absurd that, for the living, space should endure while time is erased, when space is, in fact, the depository of time, albeit a silent one, telling no tales. It's absurd that life should be like that for the living, because what comes afterwards is its polar opposite, and we are entirely unprepared for it. For now time does not pass, elapse or flow, it perpetuates itself simultaneously and in every detail, though to speak of "now" is perhaps a fallacy. That is the second worst thing, the details, because anything that we experienced or that made even the slightest impact on us when we were mortal reappears with the awful concomitant that now everything has weight and meaning: the words spoken lightly, the mechanical gestures, the accumulated afternoons of childhood parade past singly, one after the other, the effort of a whole lifetime – establishing routines that level out both days and nights – turns out to have been pointless, and each day and night is recalled with excessive clarity and singularity and with a degree of reality incongruous with our present state which knows nothing now of touch. Everything is concrete and excessive, and the razor edge of repetition becomes a torment, because the curse consists in remembering *everything*, the minutes of each hour of each day lived through, the minutes and hours and days of tedium and work and joy, of study and grief and humiliation and sleep, as well as those of waiting, which formed the greater part.

But, as I have already said, that is only the second worst thing, there is something far more wounding, which is that now I not only remember what I saw and heard and knew when I was mortal, but I remember it in its entirety, that is, including what I did not see or know or hear, even things that were beyond my grasp, but which affected me or those who were important to me, and which possibly had a hand in shaping me. You discover the full magnitude of what you only intuited while alive, all the more as you become an adult, I can't say older because I never reached old age: that you only know a fragment of what happens to you and that when you believe yourself capable of explaining or recounting what has happened to you up until a particular date, you do not have sufficient information, you do not know what other people's intentions were or the motivations behind impulses, you have no knowledge of what is hidden: the people closest to us seem like actors suddenly stepping out in front of

a theatre curtain, and we have no idea what they were doing only
a second earlier, when they were not there before us. Perhaps they
appear disguised as Othello or as Hamlet and yet the previous
moment they were smoking an impossible, anachronistic cigarette
in the wings and glancing impatiently at the watch which they
have now removed in order to seem to be someone else. Likewise,
we know nothing about the events at which we were not present
and the conversations we did not hear, those that took place
behind our back and mentioned us or criticized us or judged us
and condemned us. Life is compassionate, all lives are, at least that
is the norm, which is why we consider as wicked those people who
do not cover up or hide or lie, those who tell everything that they
know and hear, as well as what they do and think. We call them
cruel. And it is in that cruel state that I find myself now.

I see myself, for example, as a child about to fall asleep in my
bed on the countless nights of a childhood that was satisfactory or
without surprises, with my bedroom door ajar so that I could see
the light until sleep overcame me, being lulled by the voices of my
father and my mother and a guest at supper or some late arrival,
who was almost always Dr Arranz, a pleasant man who smiled a
lot and spoke in a low voice and who, to my delight, would arrive
just before I went to sleep, in time to come into my room to
see how I was, the privilege of an almost daily check-up and the
calming hand of the doctor slipping beneath your pyjama jacket,
the warm and unrepeatable hand that touches you in a way that
no one else will ever touch you again throughout your entire
life, the nervous child feeling that any anomaly or danger will be
detected by that hand and therefore stopped, it is the hand that
saves; and the stethoscope dangling from his ears and the cold,
salutary touch that your chest shrinks from, and sometimes the
handle of an inherited silver spoon engraved with initials placed
on the tongue, and which, for a moment, seems about to stick

in your throat, a feeling that would give way to relief when I remembered, after the first contact, that it was Arranz holding the spoon in his reassuring, steady hand, mistress of metallic objects, nothing could happen while he was listening to your chest or peering at you with his torch fixed on his forehead. After his brief visit and his two or three jokes – sometimes my mother would lean in the doorway waiting until he had finished examining me and making me laugh, and she would laugh too – I would feel even more at ease and would begin to fall asleep listening to their chatter in the nearby lounge, or listening to them listening for a while to the radio or playing a game of cards, at a time when time barely passed, it seems impossible because it's not that long ago, although from then until now enough time has elapsed for me to live and die. I hear the laughter of those who were still young, although I couldn't see them as young then, I can now: my father laughed the least, he was a handsome, taciturn man with a look of permanent melancholy in his eyes, perhaps because he had been a republican and had lost the war, and that is probably something you never recover from, having lost a war against your compatriots and neighbours. He was a kindly man who never got angry with me or my mother and who spent a lot of time at home writing articles and book reviews, which he tended to publish under various pseudonyms in the newspapers, because it was best not to use his own name; or perhaps reading, he was a great francophile, I mainly recall novels by Camus and Simenon. Dr Arranz was a jollier man, with a lazy, teasing way of talking, inventive and full of unusual turns-of-phrase, the kind of man children idolize because he knows how to do card tricks and comes out with unexpected rhymes and talks to them about football – then it was Kopa, Rial, Di Stefano, Puskas and Gento – and he thinks up games that will interest them and awaken their imaginations, except that, in fact, he never has time to stay and

play them for real. And my mother, always well-dressed despite
the fact that there wasn't much money in the home of one of
the war's losers – there wasn't – better dressed than my father
because she still had her own father, my grandfather, to buy her
clothes, she was slight and cheerful and sometimes looked sadly at
her husband, and always looked at me enthusiastically, later, as
you get older, not many people look at you like that either. I see
this now because I see it all complete, I see that, while I was
gradually becoming submerged in sleep, the laughter in the living
room never came from my father, and that, on the other hand, he
was the only one listening to the radio, an impossible image until
very recently, but which is now as clear as the old images which,
while I was mortal, gradually grew dimmer, more compressed
the longer I lived. I see that on some nights, Dr Arranz and my
mother went out, and now I understand all those references to
good tickets, which, in my imagination then, I always thought
of as being clipped by an usher at the football stadium or at the
bullring – those places I never went to – and to which I never
gave another thought. On other nights, there were no good
tickets and no one mentioned them, or there were rainy nights
when there was no question of going for a walk or to an open-air
dance, and now I know that then my mother and Dr Arranz
would go into the bedroom when they were sure I had gone to
sleep after having been touched on my chest and on the stomach
by the same hands that would then touch her, hands that were
no longer warm, but urgent, the hand of the doctor that calms
and probes and persuades and demands; and having been kissed
on the cheek or the forehead by the same lips that would subsequently kiss the easy-going, low voice – thus silencing it. And
whether they went to the theatre or to the cinema or to a club
or merely went into the next room, my father would listen to
the radio alone while he waited, so as not to hear anything, but

also, with the passage of time and the onset of routine – with the levelling out of nights that always happens when nights keep repeating themselves – in order to distract himself for half an hour or three quarters of an hour (doctors are always in such a hurry), because he inevitably became interested in what he was listening to. The doctor would leave without saying goodbye to him and my mother would stay in the bedroom, waiting for my father, she would put on a nightdress and change the sheets, he never found her there in her pretty skirts and stockings. I see now the conversation that began that state of affairs, which, for me, was not a cruel one but a kindly one that lasted my whole life, and, during that conversation, Dr Arranz is sporting the sharp little moustache that I noticed on the faces of lawyers in parliament until the day Franco died, and not only there, but on soldiers and notaries and bankers and lecturers, on writers and on countless doctors, not on him though, he was one of the first to get rid of it. My father and my mother are sitting in the dining room and I still have no consciousness or memory, I am a child lying in its cradle, I cannot yet walk or speak and there is no reason why I should ever have found out: she keeps her eyes lowered all the time and says nothing, he looks first incredulous and then horrified: horrified and fearful, rather than indignant. And one of the things that Arranz says is this:

"Look, León, I pass a lot of information on to the police and it never fails; basically, what I say goes. I've taken a while to get around to you but I know perfectly well what you got up to in the war, how you gave the nod to the militiamen on who to take for a ride. But even if that wasn't so, in your case, I've no need to make anything much up, I just have to stretch the facts a little, to say that you consigned to the ditch half the people in our neighbourhood wouldn't be that far from the truth, you'd have done the same to me if you could. More than ten years have

passed, but you'd still be hauled up in front of a firing squad if
I told them what I know, and I've no reason to keep quiet about
it. So it's up to you, you can either have a bit of a rough time on
my terms or you can stop having any kind of time at all, neither
good nor bad nor average."

"And what are your terms exactly?"

I see Dr Arranz gesture with his head in the direction of my
silent mother – a gesture that makes of her a thing – whom he also
knew during the war and from before, in that same neighbourhood that lost so many of its residents.

"I want to screw her. Night after night, until I get tired of it."

Arranz got tired as everyone does of everything, given time.
He got tired when I was still at an age when that essential word
did not even figure in my vocabulary, nor did I even conceive
of its meaning. My mother, on the other hand, was at the age
when she was beginning to lose her bloom and to laugh only
rarely, while my father began to prosper and to dress better, and
to sign with his own name – which was not León – the articles
and the reviews that he wrote and to lose the look of melancholy
in his clouded eyes; and to go out at night with some good tickets
while my mother stayed at home playing solitaire or listening to
the radio, or, a little later, watching television, resigned.

All those who have speculated on the afterlife or the continuing
existence of consciousness beyond death – if that is what we are,
consciousness – have not taken into account the danger or rather
the horror of remembering everything, even what we did not
know: knowing everything, everything that concerns us or that
involved us either closely or from afar. I see with absolute clarity
faces that I passed once in the street, a man I gave money to
without even glancing at him, a woman I watched in the under-
ground and whom I haven't thought of since, the features of a
postman who delivered some unimportant telegram, the figure

of a child I saw on a beach, when I too was a child. I relive the long minutes I spent waiting at airports or those spent queuing outside a museum or watching the waves on a distant beach, or packing my bags and later unpacking them, all the most tedious moments, those that are of no account and which we usually refer to as dead time. I see myself in cities I visited a long time ago, just passing through, with a few free hours to stroll around them and then wipe them from my memory: I see myself in Hamburg and in Manchester, in Basle and in Austin, places I would never have gone to if my work hadn't taken me there. I see myself too in Venice, some time ago, on honeymoon with my wife Luisa, with whom I spent those last few years of peace and contentment, I see myself in the most recent part of my life, even though it is now remote. I'm coming back from a trip and she's waiting for me at the airport, not once, all the time we were married, did she fail to come and meet me, even if I'd only been away for a couple of days, despite the awful traffic and despite all the activities we can so easily do without and which are precisely those that we find most pressing. I'd be so tired that I'd only have the strength to change television channels, the programmes are the same everywhere now anyway, while she prepared me a light supper and kept me company, looking bored but patient, knowing that after that initial torpor and the imminent night's rest, I would be fully recovered and that the following day, I would be my usual self, an energetic, jokey person who spoke in a rather low voice, in order to underline the irony that all women love, laughter runs in their veins and, if it's a funny joke, they can't help but laugh, even if they detest the person making the joke. And the following afternoon, once I'd recovered, I used to go and see María, my lover, who used to laugh even more because my jokes were still new to her.

I was always so careful not to give myself away, not to wound and to be kind, I only ever met María at her apartment so that no one would see me out with her anywhere and ask questions later on, or be cruel and tell tales, or simply wait to be introduced. Her apartment was nearby and I spent many afternoons there, though not every afternoon, on the way back to my own apartment, that meant a delay of only half an hour or three quarters of an hour, sometimes a little more, sometimes I would amuse myself looking out of her window, the window of a lover is always more interesting than our own will ever be. I never made a mistake, because mistakes in these matters reveal a sort of lack of consideration, or worse, they are acts of real cruelty. I met María once when I was out with Luisa, in a packed cinema at a première, and my lover took advantage of the crowd to come over to us and to hold my hand for a moment, as she passed by without looking at me, she brushed her familiar thigh against mine and took hold of my hand and stroked it. Luisa could not possibly have seen this or noticed or even suspected the existence of that tenuous, ephemeral, clandestine contact, but even so, I decided not to see María for a couple of weeks, after which time and after my refusing to answer the phone in my office, she called me one afternoon at home, luckily, my wife was out.

"What's wrong?" she said.

"You must never phone me here, you know that."

"I wouldn't phone you there if you'd pick up the phone in your office. I've been waiting a whole fortnight," she said.

And then, making an effort to recover the anger I had felt a fortnight before, I said:

"And I'll never pick up the phone to you again if you ever touch me when Luisa is there. Don't even think of it."

She fell silent.

You forget almost everything in life and remember everything in death, or in this cruel state which is what being a ghost is.

But in life I forgot and so I started seeing her again now and then, thanks to that process by which everything becomes indefinitely postponed for a while, and we always believe that there will continue to be a tomorrow in which it will be possible to stop what today and yesterday passes and elapses and flows, what is imperceptibly becoming another routine which, in its way, also levels out our days and our nights until they become unimaginable without all their essential elements, and the nights and days must be identical, at least in their essence, so that nothing is relinquished or sacrificed by those who want them and those who endure them. Now I remember everything and that's why I remember my death so clearly, or, rather, what I knew of my death when it happened, which was little and, indeed, nothing in comparison with all that I know now, given the constant razor edge of repetition.

I returned from one of my trips exhausted and Luisa didn't fail me, she came to meet me. We didn't talk much in the car, nor while I was mechanically unpacking my suitcase and glancing through the accumulated mail and listening to the messages on the answering machine that she had kept for my return. I was alarmed when I heard one of them, because I immediately recognized María's voice, she said my name once and was then cut off, and that made my feeling of alarm subside for a moment, the voice of a woman saying my name and then breaking off was of no significance, there was no reason why Luisa should have felt worried if she had heard it. I lay down on the bed in front of the television, changing channels, Luisa brought me some cold meat and a shop-bought dessert, she clearly had neither the time nor the inclination to make me even an omelette. It was still early, but she had turned out the light in the bedroom to help me get to sleep, and there I stayed, drowsy and peaceful, with a vague memory of her caresses, the hand that calms even when it touches your chest distractedly and possibly impatiently. Then she left the bedroom and I eventually fell asleep with the television on, at some point, I stopped changing channels.

I don't know how much time passed, no, that's not true, since now I know exactly, I enjoyed seventy-three minutes of deep sleep and of dreams that all took place in foreign parts, whence I had once again returned safe and sound. Then I woke up and I saw the bluish light of the television, the light illuminating the foot of the bed, rather than any actual images, because I didn't have time. I see and I saw rushing towards me something black and heavy and doubtless as cold as a stethoscope, but it was violent rather than salutary. It fell once only to be raised again, and in those tenths of a second before it came crashing down a second time, already spattered with blood, I thought that Luisa must be killing me because of that message which had said only my name and then broken off and perhaps there had been many other things that she had erased after listening to them all, leaving only the beginning for me to listen to on my return, a mere foreshadowing of what was killing me. The black thing fell again and this time it killed me, and my last conscious thought was not to put up any resistance, to make no attempt to stop it because it was unstoppable and perhaps too because it didn't seem such a bad death, to die at the hands of the person with whom I had lived in peace and contentment, and without ever hurting each other until, that is, we finally did. It's a tricky word to use, and can easily be misconstrued, but perhaps I came to feel that my death was a just death.

I see this now and I see the whole thing, with an afterwards and a before, although the afterwards does not, strictly speaking, concern me and is therefore not so painful. But the before is, or rather the rebuttal of what I glimpsed and half-thought between the lowering and the raising and the lowering again of the black thing that finished me off. Now I can see Luisa talking to a man I don't know and who has a moustache like the one Dr Arranz wore in his day, not a slim moustache, though, but soft and thick and with a few grey hairs. He's middle-aged, as I was and as perhaps Luisa was, although she always seemed young to me, just as my parents or Arranz never did. They are in the living room of an unfamiliar apartment, his apartment, a ramshackle place, full of books and paintings and ornaments, a very mannered apartment. The man is called Manolo Reyna and he has enough money never to have to dirty his hands. It is the afternoon and they are sitting on a sofa, talking in whispers, and at that moment I am visiting María, two weeks before my death on the return from a trip, and that trip has still not begun, they are still making their preparations. The whispers are clearly audible, they have a degree of reality which seems incongruous now, not with my current non-tactile state, but with life itself, in which nothing is ever quite so concrete, in which nothing ever breathes quite so much. There is a moment, though, when Luisa raises her voice, like someone raising their voice to defend themselves or to defend someone else, and what she says is this:

"But he's always been so good to me, I've nothing to reproach him with, and that's what's so difficult."

And Manolo Reyna answers slowly:

"It wouldn't be any easier or any more difficult if he had made your life impossible. When it comes to killing someone, it doesn't matter any more what they've done, it always seems an extreme response to any kind of behaviour."

I see Luisa put her thumb to her mouth and bite it a little, a gesture I've so often seen her make when she's uncertain, or, rather, before making a decision. It's a trivial gesture and it's unseemly that it should also appear in the midst of a conversation we were not party to, the one that takes place behind our backs

and mentions us or criticizes us or even defends us, or judges us
and condemns us to death.

"Well, you kill him, then; you can't expect me to do anything
that extreme."

Now I see that the person standing next to my television
set – still on – and wielding the black thing is not Luisa, nor even
Manolo Reyna with his folkloric name, but someone contracted
and paid to do it, to strike me twice on the forehead, the word
is assassin, in the war a lot of militiamen were used for such
purposes. My assassin hits me twice and does so quite dispassionately, and that death no longer seems to me just or appropriate
or, of course, compassionate, as life usually is, and as mine was.
The black thing is a hammer with a wooden shaft and an iron
head, a common-or-garden hammer. It belongs in my apartment,
I recognize it.

There where time passes and flows, a lot of time has gone by,
so much so that no one whom I knew or met or pitied or loved
remains. Each one of them, I suppose, will return unnoticed to
that space in which forgotten times past accumulate, and they
will see only strangers, new men and women who, like children,
believe that the world began with their birth and there's no
point asking them about our past, erased existence. Now Luisa
will remember and will know everything that she did not know in
life or at my death. I cannot speak now of nights and days, everything has been levelled out without resort to effort or routine,
a routine in which I can say that I knew, above all, peace and
contentment: when I was mortal, all that time ago, in that place
where there still is time.

EVERYTHING BAD COMES BACK

For the night doctor,
who did not want to remain fictitious

TODAY I RECEIVED a letter that reminded me of a friend. It was written by a woman unknown both to myself and to that friend.

I met him fifteen or sixteen years ago and – for no other reason than that he died – stopped seeing him two years ago, not that we ever saw each other with any frequency, given that he lived in Paris and I in Madrid. Although he visited my city only rarely, I used to visit his quite often. However, we first met in neither of those two cities, but in Barcelona, and before that meeting, I had previously read a book of his sent to me by a Madrid publishing house I used to work for as a reader (work, as is usually the case, that was poorly remunerated). There was little likelihood of this novel, or whatever it was, ever being published and I can remember almost nothing about it, except that it revealed a certain inventiveness with words, a strong rhythmic sense and a broad culture (for example, the author knew the word "wrack") but apart from that it was more or less unintelligible, at least to me. Were I a critic, I would have described him as out-Joycing Joyce, though he was less puerile, or perhaps senile, than the later Joyce, to which his own work bore only a remote resemblance.

Nevertheless, I recommended the book for publication and expressed my qualified regard for it in my report. His agent subsequently phoned me (for this writer, whose true vocation seemed to be to remain forever unpublished, nonetheless had an agent) to arrange a meeting to coincide with a trip his client would be making to Barcelona, where his family lived and where, fifteen or sixteen years ago, I too was living.

His name was Xavier Comella and I never did ascertain whether the business to which he sometimes referred vaguely as "the family business" was in fact the chain of clothes shops of the same name in Barcelona (selling mainly sweaters). Given the iconoclastic nature of his writing, I was expecting some wild, bearded individual, some kind of visionary with a penchant for pendants and vaguely Polynesian clothes, but he wasn't like that at all. The man who emerged from the exit of the Metro at Tibidabo, where we'd arranged to meet, was only slightly older than myself, I was about twenty-eight or twenty-nine at the time, and much better dressed (I'm a very neat person myself, but he was wearing a tie – with a small knot – and cufflinks, unusual in men of our age and particularly so then); and he had an extraordinarily old-fashioned face, a face – like his writing – straight out of the interwar period. He wore his slightly wavy, blondish hair combed back, like a fighter pilot or a French actor in a black-and-white movie – Gérard Philipe or the young Jean Marais – and his sherry-brown eyes had a small dark fleck in the white of the left one, which gave his gaze a wounded look. He had good, robust teeth and a well-defined jaw so firm it gave the impression of being permanently clenched. His very prominent cranium, the bones of which were clearly visible beneath the smooth brow, always seemed on the point of exploding, not because of its unusual size, but because the taut skin over the frontal bone seemed incapable of containing it, or perhaps that was just the effect of the two vertical veins at his temples that seemed somehow too protuberant, too blue. He was good-looking, genial and, moreover, extraordinarily polite, especially for a man of his age and given the rather boorish times we lived in. He was one of those men you know you will never be able to confide in, but one in whom you can confidently trust. He had a studiedly foreign, or rather, extraterritorial look about him that only emphasized his estrangement from the times he'd been born into, a look acquired no doubt during the seven or eight years he'd spent out of Spain. He spoke Spanish with the attractive pronunciation of Catalans who have never actually spoken much Catalan (with soft c's and z's, soft g's and j's) and with the slight hint of a stammer at the beginning of sentences, occasionally stumbling over the first three or four words, as if he had to perform some minor mental act of translation. He could speak and read several languages, including Latin, in fact he mentioned that he'd been reading Ovid's *Tristia* on the plane from Paris, and he said this without a trace of pedantry but rather with the satisfaction of one who has mastered some difficult task. He possessed a certain degree of worldly wisdom which he enjoyed showing off; during the long conversation we had in the bar of a nearby hotel, we talked almost exclusively about literature and painting and music, that is, about highly forgettable things, but he did tell me something of his life, about which he always spoke – on that occasion and during all the years we knew each other – with a contradictory blend of discretion and shamelessness. By that I mean that he was prepared to reveal everything or nearly everything, even about very intimate matters, but he always did so with a kind of grave artlessness – or was it perhaps tact? – which, in a way, diminished their importance, like someone who considers that all the strange, sad, terrible, agonizing things that happen to him are perfectly normal, a fate shared by everyone and so, presumably, by the person listening, who will not, therefore, be surprised by what he hears. Not that Xavier eschewed the confessional gesture, but he resorted to it, perhaps, more because he saw it as part of the gestural repertoire of the tormented than because he had any real awareness of what is, at least in principle, untellable. On that first occasion, he told me the following: he'd studied medicine but never practised as a doctor, instead living a life dedicated entirely to literature, funded by a generous inheritance or by some kind of private income, possibly – I can't quite remember now – from a grandfather who owned a textile factory. Whatever the origin of the money, he enjoyed the use of it and had lived off it for the seven or eight years he'd spent in Paris – a move indeed made possible by that money – fleeing from what he considered to be the mediocrity and flaccidity of intellectual life in Barcelona, which, given how young he was when he left, he really only knew about through the press. (Although he grew up in Barcelona, he was born in Madrid, where his mother came from.)

In Paris he'd married a woman called Eliane (he always referred to her by name, I never once heard him call her "my wife"), who, according to him, had the most exquisite colour sense he'd ever come across in a fellow human being (I didn't ask at the time, but I presumed that she must be a painter). He had a wide-ranging and ambitious literary plan of which, he remarked precisely, he had so far completed about twenty per cent, although none of it had as yet been published. Apart from the people closest to him, I was the first person to have shown any interest in his writings, which comprised novels, essays, sonnets and plays, even a play for puppets. He obviously thought that my opinion held considerable sway at the head office of the publishing house, not realizing that mine was only one voice amongst many and, given my youth, far from being one of the most influential. He gave me the impression that he was reasonably happy, whatever that means: he seemed to be very much in love with his wife; he was living in Paris whereas, in Spain, we were only just getting over Franco, or so people said; he didn't have to work, his only obligations being those he imposed upon himself; and he doubtless enjoyed a pleasant and interesting social life. And yet, even at our first meeting, I sensed something turbulent and uneasy about him, as if he were surrounded by a cloud of suffering, like a cloud of dust, that gradually gathered about him only to be shaken off afterwards and left behind. When he described to me the amount of work he put into his writing, the endless hours spent labouring over every one of those pages I had read, I thought it was nothing more than that, a concept of writing as old-fashioned as he was himself, a concept that was almost "pathetic", in the original sense of that word: a summoning up of the pain required to make words, regardless of meaning, communicate intense emotion, the way, he said, that music or pure colour do, or the way mathematics is supposed to. I asked him if he'd also spent hours on one of his rather easier pages to remember, which consisted of the word "riding" repeated five times on each line, thus:

riding riding riding riding riding

He looked at me with ingenuous eyes, surprised, and then, after a few seconds, he burst out laughing: "No," he said, "of course I didn't." Then he added, with unexpected simplicity: "You do say some funny things," and started laughing again.

He was always rather slow on the uptake when it came to the jokes or, rather, the gentle leg-pulls I allowed myself, especially later on, simply as a way of lessening the intensity of whatever he was telling me. It was as if he didn't immediately understand the ironic register, as if that too required translation, but then, after a few seconds of bewilderment or assimilation, he would laugh out loud – his laughter was almost femininely openhearted – as if amazed that anyone were capable of making a joke in the middle of a serious, not to say solemn or even dramatic, conversation, and he really appreciated it, both the joke and the capability. This is often the case with people who believe they haven't an ounce of frivolity in them; he did, he simply didn't know it. When I saw his reaction, I ventured another funny remark (I should perhaps explain that this is my principal way of demonstrating my liking and affection for someone), and later I said to him: "The only thing that's lacking for your life to be idyllic, the sort of life led by characters in a Scott Fitzgerald story before everything turns sour, is for one of your books to be published." His face darkened slightly at this and I thought that perhaps this was caused by my mention of Fitzgerald, an author who was of even less interest to him than he was to me. He answered me gravely: "It's more a question of excess than lack." He paused theatrically, as if debating whether or not to tell me what he was clearly burning to say. I kept silent. So did he (he could withstand silence better than anyone I knew); I broke first. I said: "What do you mean?" He waited a little longer before replying and then announced: "I suffer from melancholia." "Well, I never," I said, unable to suppress a smile, "people who suffer from that are usually people who feel they're over-privileged. But it's such a very ancient illness, it can't be that serious, nothing classical ever is, wouldn't you agree?"

There was rarely any ambiguity in what he said and he hastened to clear up what he judged to have been a misunderstanding. "I suffer, more or less continually, from depressive melancholia," he said. "I'm on medication all the time. That keeps it under control, but if I stopped taking the medication, I would almost certainly kill myself. I already tried to do so once, before I came to live in Paris. It wasn't that any particular misfortune had befallen me, I was just in such terrible mental pain that I couldn't bear to go on living. That could happen to me again at any moment and would happen were I to stop taking the medication. At least that's what they tell me and I imagine they're probably right, after all, I'm a doctor too." He wasn't being melodramatic, he spoke about it quite dispassionately, in the same tone in which he'd told me about everything else. "What happened?" I asked. "I was staying at my father's country house in Gerona, near Cassá de la Selva. I aimed a rifle at my chest, holding the rifle butt between my knees. My hands started shaking, I lost my grip, and the bullet embedded itself in a wall instead. I was too young," he added, by way of an excuse, and gave me an amiable smile. He was a very considerate man and insisted on paying the bill.

*

We began writing to each other and met whenever I visited Paris. I went there, in order to get over some upset or other, only a few months after our first meeting. I used to stay with an Italian friend, a woman whom I've always found amusing and who has, therefore, always been a source of consolation to me. At the time, the company of Xavier Comella simply interested and entertained me, later it became something that demanded repetition, as happens with those people one comes to count on, even in their absence.

At the time, Xavier was living in his father-in-law's house with his wife Eliane, who was French by birth but Chinese in appearance. She was almost depressingly delicate in the way oriental women are who pride themselves on their refinement, and she was certainly refined. Her fantastic colour sense, so highly praised by her husband, was not deployed on any canvas, but in interior design, although it seemed to me that, up until then, she'd worked mainly on the houses of friends and acquaintances rather than for actual clients, as well as on the design of the restaurant owned by her father, Xavier's father-in-law, a restaurant I never visited but which, according to Xavier, was "the finest Chinese restaurant in France", not that that's saying very much. When he was with his wife, the natural attentiveness of this man who was in the process of becoming my friend became so exaggerated that, at times, it proved positively irritating: he would ask me not to smoke because cigarette smoke made her feel sick; in cafés we always had to sit out on the covered terraces both to avoid the cigarette smoke and because the air circulated more freely there; we also had to sit so that her back was to the pavement, because the sight of the traffic made her dizzy; we could never go anywhere, not even to a cinema that was even half full, because Eliane was afraid of crowds, nor of course could we ever go to a cellar bar or a night club because that gave her claustrophobia; we also had to avoid any large open spaces, such as the Place Vendôme, because she suffered equally badly from agoraphobia; she couldn't walk or remain standing for any longer than it takes for the lights to change and, if there was a queue at the theatre or a museum, even if it was only for a matter of minutes, Xavier would have to accompany Eliane to the nearest café and deposit her there – having first checked that there was no other threat to her safety (this took some time since the threats were so various) – in order that she could wait, seated and safe. What with one thing and another, by the time he got back to me in the queue to keep me company in my slow advance, I'd already got the tickets and we had to go back and find her. By then, of course, she would have ordered some tea and we would have to wait while she drank it. On more than one occasion the show began without us or we were obliged to go round the museum at lightning speed. Going out with the two of them together was rather trying, not only because of all these obligations and inconveniences, but also because adoration is never

a pretty sight, still less so when the person doing the adoring is a
person for whom one feels a certain regard. It inspires a sense
of shame, of embarrassment and, in the case of Xavier Comella,
it was like being present at a display – albeit partial – of the most
deeply felt corner of his private life, something we can tolerate
only in ourselves – just as we can only bear the sight of our
own blood, our own nail clippings. And it was perhaps all the
more embarrassing because, when you met Eliane, you could
understand, or at least imagine, why he felt that way. It wasn't
that she was an extraordinary beauty, nor was she exactly talkative
(of course, she never asked for or complained about anything
because that would have been out of keeping with her refined
nature, neither was it necessary: Xavier was a solicitous and
punctilious interpreter of her every need). My memory of her
is of an utterly vague figure, but her principal charm – which
was considerable – probably lay in the fact that, even when she
was there before you, she felt like a memory, a blurred and
tenuous memory and, as such, harmonious and peaceful, sooth-
ing and faintly nostalgic, impossible to grasp. Holding her in
your arms must have been like embracing something one has
lost, as sometimes happens in dreams. Xavier told me once that
he'd been in love with her since he was fourteen years old, I didn't
dare ask how or where they'd met at such a tender age, but
then I don't ask many questions. A single image of the two of
them together predominates over all the others. One morning,
we visited an open-air market selling flowers and plants; it began
to rain really rather hard, but because the excursion had been
specially arranged so that Eliane could buy, amongst other things,
the first peonies of the year, no one even considered looking
for shelter, not that there was any, instead Xavier opened his
umbrella and took enormous pains to ensure that not a single
drop of rain fell on her as she continued on her meticulous and

unalterable course, with Xavier following always a couple of paces behind, holding his waterproof vault above her and getting soaked in the process, like a devoted servant inured to such things. I brought up the rear, umbrella-less but not daring to abandon the cortège, like a servant of a lower rank, less committed and quite unrewarded.

When she was not with us, he was more forthcoming, much more than he was in his letters too, which were affectionate but restrained, indeed at times they were so intensely laconic that – like the taut skin and the swollen veins on his forehead – they seemed to presage some explosion, an explosion that would take place outside the envelope, in real life. It was during such a meeting, when Eliane was not with us, that he first spoke to me of the violent rages to which he was subject and which I always found so hard to imagine given that, over the thirteen or fourteen years I knew him, I was never a witness to one, although it's true that we saw each other only infrequently and that his life seems to me now like a defective copy of a book, full of blank pages, or like a city that one has driven through many times before but always at night. Once he told me about a recent visit to Barcelona and how he'd borne in silence for as long as he could his father's absurd words of advice – his father was separated from Xavier's mother and had remarried – and how, then, in a sudden fit of rage, he'd started wrecking the house, hurling furniture against walls, tearing down chandeliers, ripping up paintings, demolishing shelves and, of course, kicking in the television set. No one stopped him; he simply calmed down of his own accord after a few cataclysmic minutes. He took no pleasure in telling me this, but neither did he show any regret or sorrow. I met his father in Paris together with his new Dutch wife, who wore a diamond stud in her nose (a woman ahead of her time). His father's name was Ernest and the only thing he had in common with Xavier was the prominent forehead: he was much taller and had black hair with not a trace of grey in it, possibly dyed, he was a vain man, indulgent and easy-going, but slightly disdainful of his own son, whom he evidently didn't take at all seriously, although that may not have meant much, since he obviously didn't take anything very seriously. He was like an eternal spoiled child, still keen on riding competitions, skeet shooting and – at the time – leafing through treatises on Hindu philosophy; he was one of those people, increasingly rare nowadays, who seemed to spend his entire life lounging around in a silk dressing gown. Xavier didn't take his father very seriously either, but he couldn't treat him with the same disdain, partly because his father irritated him so much, but also because he just hadn't inherited that particular characteristic.

It was on another occasion when Eliane was absent, about two or three years after our first meeting, that Xavier told me about the death of their newborn child, possibly, I can't quite remember, strangled by its own umbilical cord, but no, it wasn't that, because I recall now one of his extremely rare remarks on the subject (he hadn't even told me they were expecting a baby): "It's much worse for Eliane than it is for me," he said. "I don't know how she's going to react. The worst thing is that the child did actually live, so we can't just forget about it, we'd already given it a name." I didn't ask him what that name was, so that I wouldn't have to remember it too. Years later, talking about something else entirely – but perhaps not thinking about that something else – he wrote to me: "There is nothing more repellent than having to bury something that has only just been born." He had still not separated from Eliane – or Eliane from him – when he spoke to me one day about a literary project of his that would require an experiment. He said: "I'm going to write an essay on pain. I thought at first that I'd make it a strictly medical treatise and entitle it *Pain, Anaesthesia and Diathesis*, but I want to go beyond that. What really interests me about pain is its mystery, its ethical nature and how to describe it in words, all of which is easily within my grasp. I've decided that in a few days' time I'll stop taking the medication for my depression and see what happens, see how long I can bear it, and simply observe the process of my mental pain, which always ends up taking on various physical manifestations, the worst of which are the excruciating migraines. The term 'migraine' always seems to be taken rather lightly, doubtless because of that old joke about headaches and dissatisfied wives, but it actually describes one of the greatest sufferings known to man. There is a possibility that if I want to stop the experiment at some point, it might already be too late, but I can't not do this research." Xavier Comella had continued to write – novels, poetry and an epistemology, as well as what he called "night watches". Of all this work, the only piece we'd finally managed to get accepted for publication, by the Madrid publishing house that had brought us together in the first place, was his novel *Vivisection*, a much longer book than the one I'd read. Nevertheless, owing to endless delays, it had still not seen the light of day, and he was now working on a translation of Burton's *Anatomy of Melancholy*, commissioned by the same publishing house, who had chosen him for the task partly because of his profession. He was, therefore, still an unpublished author and, from time to time, he would despair, decide that he wanted to remain unpublished and cancel contracts only to have them drawn up all over again at a later date. Fortunately, his publisher was a patient man, both kindly and prepared to take risks, a combination almost unknown in the publishing world. "Aren't you curious to see your book in print?" I asked. "Of course I am," he replied, "but I can't wait. Besides," he added, with his usual precision, "once I've finished the essay on pain, I'll have completed sixty per cent of my work." I said: "The day we met, you told me that without the medication you'd probably kill yourself and, if that happened, you'd only have completed fifty per cent, perhaps less, depending on the percentage you give your essay. And fifty per cent really isn't very much, is it?" He gave that delayed laugh of his and said, slipping into the oddly naive idiom he occasionally resorted to: "Honestly, the things you come out with . . ." I didn't feel particularly worried, since I'd always believed that he was exaggerating when he described the more dramatic and spectacular incidents in his life.

Over the following months, his letters became even more austere than usual and his childish writing more of a hasty scribble. Only at the end of those letters would he add a few words about himself or his state of health or about how his experiment was going: "At the present time, the maximum speed at which we are travelling towards the future remains insufficient and we grow old not with respect to the future but with respect to our past. My future perfect can't wait to arrive, my past perfect is unstoppable." Or: "I've always lived with the fear that one day I would have to fall silent, for good. As you see, my friend, I'm more of a coward than ever." But shortly after that, he wrote: "Every day I grow more invulnerable inside and more combustible outside." And later on again: "The most heroic quality in man is not perhaps to live or to die but to endure." And in the letter following that: "What will they think of us? What do we think of ourselves? What will you think of me? I don't want to know. But the questions provoke a slight feeling of depression. That's all." "As I said to you in the course of our conversation outside the Jardin du Luxembourg," he said once, referring to the work he was about to embark upon, "my way into the subject entails provoking a relapse into endogenous colic and when the meandering route followed by my first seventy

commentaries leads you at last to the final one, you will understand the reason why, especially if you remember what I told
you about the exceptional circumstances of my illness. This new
descent into Hades is a touch foolish and I'd be the first to
reproach myself with that, but why fish for tuna when you
could be catching shark?" And later: "I'm not ill *again*. It's a
continuation of the same illness." He had to abandon the experiment sooner than expected. He'd estimated that it would take
six months to reach crisis point but, after only a month, he had
to be hospitalized for two weeks, unable to carry on without his
medication and still without enough material to start writing. I
know that both his family and his doctors rebuked him sharply.

Shortly after this, he suffered a series of setbacks and changes
in his life, although he informed me of them only gradually,
doubtless out of a sense of tact. He only told me that he'd
separated from Eliane some time after it had happened. He
didn't explain anything to me outright but, during a conversation – this time in Madrid where he was on a visit to a brother
who'd moved there – he implied that there were four reasons:
the death of a child doesn't necessarily bring people together, it
can also drive them apart if the face of the other is a constant
reminder of the death of that child; the years of waiting for
something concrete to happen – a book and its publication – can
be shattered when the long-awaited event actually takes place;
whilst anything that begins in childhood is never truly over,
neither does it ever truly reach fulfilment; with regard to your
own pain, you have no option but to put up with it, what you
can't do is to expect us to watch while you inflict pain on yourself,
because we will never accept it as necessary. The break-up of
his marriage did not, of course, mean the end of his adoration:
Xavier hoped that the divorce would take a long time and that
Eliane would stay on in Paris, even though she'd been offered

an excellent job as an interior designer in Montreal.

Later on, he told me that the inheritance or private income he lived on had dried up (perhaps his father had been diverting money from the family business but had now grown tired of doing so). Up until then, Xavier's only paid work had been his monumental translation of Burton's *Anatomy of Melancholy*, of which he had still not completed even fifty per cent; he had no concept of schedules nor, of course, of getting up early. However, he decided to return to his original, neglected profession and took the necessary steps to do so in Paris, which he still had no desire to leave as long as Eliane remained there. While he waited to be given French nationality and to have his qualifications validated, he had to work as a nurse and, subsequently, in a clinic ("men and women, old people and adolescents, like so much plumbing: I go there to arbitrate amongst the horrors and the trivia"). He almost joined Médecins du Monde or Médecins sans Frontières, organizations that would have sent him off to Africa or to Central America for a while, with all expenses paid but with no salary, which would have meant returning with empty pockets. Now that he couldn't spend all his free time writing, the pace at which he was able to work towards his famous one hundred per cent had slowed considerably. He didn't much like talking about Eliane, he preferred to talk about other women, young and not so young, amongst them my Italian friend to whom I'd introduced him some years before. According to his version of events, she'd been very cruel to him; according to her version, she'd simply acted in self-defence. It seems that after spending one night together, he'd left her house only to return a few hours later with his luggage, all set to move in. She threw him out in high female dudgeon. I listened to both versions and offered no opinion, merely regretting that it had happened.

He was now no longer an unpublished author but, as expected, his novel didn't sell in Spain and was reviewed almost nowhere. When I went to Paris, we used to arrange to have supper or lunch at Balzar or at Lipp, and that didn't change, but now he allowed me to pay for him whereas before, he'd always imposed the law of hospitality: you're a stranger and you're in my city. He still dressed well – I remember he often wore a particularly smart raincoat – as if that were something his breeding would not allow him to give up; it was, perhaps, the only characteristic he'd inherited from his father. Now, however, the colours he wore were not so splendidly coordinated, as if that had always been dependent on Eliane's exquisite taste in anything to do with adornment. He mentioned her only once in a letter: "From the severed root with Eliane furious lightning shoots sprout forth, draining away half my life." We didn't see each other for two years and when I saw him again after that time, his physical appearance had changed somewhat and, with his usual tact, he forewarned me: "I'm not only worn out mentally, I'm also in terrible physical shape. A witness to this is the galloping alopecia that obliges me to wear a cap to protect me from the ill-tempered autumns we get in this part of the world." He'd had to move to a largely North African quarter. On one of my trips to Paris, I phoned him but got no reply, although I knew he was in town. Thinking that perhaps his phone had been cut off, I caught the Metro and arrived at his remote and unfamiliar new house, or rather, what turned out to be a room, tiny and sparsely furnished, a final desolate stopping place. But, in fact, all I remember of that scene was the look of happiness on his face when he opened the door to me. On his desk was a glass of wine.

*

Things improved for him somewhat while I was away, travelling to Italy rather than to Paris. Xavier had at last found the perfect job for his purposes, although, accordingly, it earned him little money: he got a job as a locum in a hospital, working more or less only when he wanted or needed to. As long as he worked a certain minimum number of hours per month, he could then increase those hours depending on how energetic he was feeling and on how much money he needed and this freed him to hurry impatiently on towards the completion of his literary work. I never really understood this impatience, bearing in mind that, since *Vivisection*, nothing else of his had been published. His novel *Hecate*, the book entitled *The Edgeless Sword*, his *Treatise on the Will*, the poems he sometimes sent me, none of these was ever successful in finding a publisher. I remember two lines from one of his "night watches": "The wakefulness of your geminate soul/is the sleep which I, mere body, deny myself." Whilst everything he wrote remained extremely obscure, it nevertheless had a certain verve. I read very little of what he was writing and he was still engaged on translating Burton's *Anatomy of Melancholy*.

One morning – by then we'd known each other for about ten or eleven years – we were once again sitting on the covered terrace of a café in St-Germain. He'd acquired a certain nobility of appearance and had discovered a way of combing his thinning hair, which did not look thin so much as lighter in colour. He seemed in good spirits after the misfortunes of recent years and he told me about the enormous progress he'd made in his writing. He had, he said, borrowing my ironic tone, completed eighty-three point five per cent of his entire body of work. Then he put on his confidential face and grew more serious: he had only two texts to complete now, a novel to be entitled *Saturn* and the long-postponed essay on pain. Given the novel's technical complexities, he would leave that to last and he now felt strong enough to return to his experiment and again stop taking his medication. He thought that, this time, he'd be able to last out long enough and be able to start writing as soon as he'd learned whatever it was he needed to learn. "Over the past few years working in my profession I've seen a lot of pain, I've even controlled it; I've both fought it and permitted it, according to what was in the patient's best interests; I've suppressed it completely with morphine, as well as with other medications and drugs that can't be found on the open market and to which only doctors have access. Many are as closely guarded as state secrets; what you can buy in pharmacies and dispensaries is only a tiny fraction of what's available, but there's a black market in everything. I've seen pain now, I've observed it, gauged it, measured it, but now it's my turn to suffer it again, and not only physical pain, which is commonplace enough, but psychic pain, the pain that makes the thinking brain want only to stop thinking, but it can't. I'm convinced that consciousness is the source of man's greatest suffering and there's no cure for it, no way to blunt it, the only end is death, though even that you can't be sure of." This time I didn't try to dissuade him, not even in the oblique, jokey way I had when he first announced his intention of embarking on this personal research. We had too much respect for each other and so I just said: "Well, keep me posted."

I can't honestly say that he did, in that he didn't keep me informed of his progress or of his thoughts on the subject, perhaps because he could only talk about it indirectly, by describing feelings and symptoms and states of mind, which he didn't in the least mind discussing and so, in the letters I received in subsequent months – I was commuting between Madrid and Italy at the time – he never said much about what was happening to him or what he was thinking, his letters were even more laconic than usual, but he did sometimes let slip the occasional disquieting remark – explicit or enigmatic, confessional or cryptic, depending

on the context. I've just today been re-reading some remarks of
his that fall into the second category, remarks that usually came
at the end of his letters, just before he signed off or even after that,
in a postscript: "Pain thought pleasure and future are the four
numbers necessary for and sufficient to my interest." "Nothing
sullies one more than an excess of modesty: pay up rather than
be your own Shylock." "Let's just do our best not to fall off the
back of the train." "If you don't desert the desert, the desert will
desert you, not in the sense that it will leave you, but in the sense
that it will make a desert of you." "Best wishes and don't let
anyone have it easy. They might make you pay for it." That's the
sort of thing he wrote. There was more of a sense of continuity,
even a kind of progress, in the first category of remarks: "I don't
feel like writing, I don't feel like working or travelling or thinking
or even despairing," he said and then, in the next letter: "I read
so as to give some semblance of being occupied." Some time
afterwards, I thought that perhaps he'd recovered slightly, for
he spoke openly – for the first time – of the experiment on which
he was engaged: "As for my ethical experiment in endogenous
pain, I'm still waiting for the explosion of the time bomb I set
ticking at the beginning of summer, but I don't know the day
or the hour it's due to go off. You see how things are, but don't
waste too much time thinking about it, it's too pathetic to merit
any deep consideration, and if there can be said to be something
titanic about all this, the truth is that I feel more like a midget."
I don't know what I wrote in reply nor if I even asked him about
it, for we forget what's in our own letters the moment we put
them in the letter box, or even before that, while we're still licking
the envelope and sealing it down. He continued to give me only
the bare outlines of his inactivity: "A bit of medicine, very little
wielding of the pen, rather more withdrawal. Dead wet leaves." I
remembered that, on his first and failed attempt, he'd mentioned

a period of six months as the time he would need to go without his medication in order to achieve what he was after, and so, with the arrival of winter, I expected that his time bomb would either explode or he'd have to stop the experiment, even if that meant being rushed into hospital again. But that season only contributed to a worsening of his suffering, which he nevertheless still judged to be insufficient: "For two months now I've been more dead than alive. I don't write, don't read, don't listen, don't see. I hear the distant rumble of thunder but I don't know if the storm is approaching or moving off, whether it's in the future or in the past. I'll close now: the vulture is already pecking at my left hemisphere." I assumed he was referring to the migraine tormenting him.

Another two months passed by with hardly any news and, at the end of that time, I received a phone call in Madrid from Eliane. After their separation I'd lost all contact with her but I still couldn't manage to feel surprised, instead I immediately thought the worst. "Xavier asked me to call you," she said, and since there was no indication as to when that had happened, I wasn't sure whether he'd asked her to do so before he died or if he'd asked her that very moment, assuming he was still alive. "He suffered a serious relapse and he's in hospital, possibly for some time, but he can't write to you for the moment and he didn't want you to worry too much. He's been very ill, but he's better now." Her words were as acceptably conventional as one would expect in such a phone call, but I did manage to ask her two things, even though that meant obliging a memory, that is, someone who was a memory twice over, to speak: "Did he try to kill himself?" "No," she replied, "it wasn't that, but he has been very ill." "Are you going to go back to him?" "No," she replied, "that's not possible."

During the final two years of our friendship, Xavier and I wrote and saw each other less frequently, I only went to Paris once and he never again visited Madrid. He often either neglected to answer my letters or took a long time to reply, and everything requires a certain rhythm. There are other things I could say about him, but I don't want to talk about them now, they're not things I actually experienced. The last time we saw each other was on a very brief trip I made to Paris. We had lunch at Balzar; he'd got a bit fatter – his chest had filled out – and it rather suited him. He smiled a lot like someone for whom going out to lunch is something of an event. He told me cautiously and briefly that, during our silence, he'd finally written his essay on pain. He said he felt sure it would be published, but said nothing about the text itself. Now he was working, continuously but with enormous difficulty, on his last book, *Saturn*. It all felt rather remote: for me, his life had become even more fragmentary, more spectral, as if, on the final pages of the defective book, there was now only punctuation, or as if I'd begun to feel that he too were merely a memory or some fictitious character. Although he was almost bald by then, his face was still handsome. I remember thinking that the veins on his forehead, even more prominent now, stood out like high relief. We said goodbye there, in rue des Écoles.

After that, I received only one letter and a telegram. The former I received after some months had passed and in it he said: "I'm not writing because I've finally got something to say to you, but simply because time passes and every day leaves me with less to say. Nothing positive. A horrible winter, full of recesses filled by swirling whirlwinds. Sediment and chaos. A dematerializing silence from my publishers. Divorce from Eliane. And a feeling of nausea as regards any creative work. Last week was filled by a coagulating tedium. The night before last was even worse: I was woken by a scream, my own." And the postscript said: "So I will darken for only a little while longer this my ash-grey matter."

I didn't feel particularly worried by this and I didn't bother to reply because in two weeks' time I would be going to Paris anyway. That was a little over two years ago. I'd already been in the city for three days, staying as usual with my Italian friend, and I still hadn't phoned Xavier, wanting to get my business in Paris over with first. On the third day I returned to the house of that Italian friend, the one who had been cruel to him or who had acted in self-defence, and she told me of his voluntary death the day before yesterday. This time he wasn't too young, this time he didn't miss; he was a doctor, he was precise; and he avoided all pain. Some days later, I managed to phone his mother, whom I never met. She told me that Xavier had completed *Saturn* two nights before the day he died (his one hundred per cent: he had reached the end of his life when he reached the end of the page). He'd made two copies and had written three letters, which were found on the table next to a glass of wine: a letter to her, a letter to his unsuccessful agent and a letter to Eliane. In the letter to his mother he'd explained the whole ritual: he would read for a while, listen to a bit of music and drink some wine before going to bed. Over the phone she was unable to tell me what music he'd listened to or what he'd read, and I never asked her again, so as not to have to remember that as well. Of the more than one thousand pages of Burton's *Anatomy of Melancholy*, he'd trans-lated only seven hundred – seventy-two per cent – and the rest still awaits someone to finish the task. I don't know what happened to his essay on pain.

The telegram I found on my return to Madrid. This is what it said: "EVERYTHING GOOD GOES NOTHING GOES WELL EVERYTHING BAD COMES BACK YOURS XAVIER."

Today I received a letter that reminded me of this friend. It was written by a woman unknown both to myself and to him.

FEWER SCRUPLES

I WAS SO strapped for cash that, two days earlier, I'd gone for a screen test for a porn movie and was amazed to see how many other women aspired to one of those roles with absolutely no dialogue, or, rather, only exclamations. I'd gone there feeling shy and embarrassed, telling myself that my daughter had to eat, that it was no big deal and that it was unlikely that the film would be seen by anyone I knew, although I know that everyone always ends up finding out about everything that happens. I doubt, though, that I'll ever be important enough in future to merit being blackmailed about my past. Besides, there's quite enough material for that already.

When I saw the queues inside the house, up the stairs and in the waiting room (the screen tests, like the filming, were being held in a three-storey house, somewhere around Torpedero Tucumán, not an area I know), I began to feel afraid that they wouldn't choose me, when, up until then, my real fear had been that they would, and my real hope that they wouldn't; that they wouldn't think I was pretty enough, or well enough endowed. There was no chance of that, I've always turned heads, all my life, I'm not exaggerating, it's true, not that it's done me much good.

"I probably won't get this job either," I thought when I saw all the other female hopefuls. "Unless the film includes a massive orgy scene and they need loads of extras." There were a lot of girls my age and younger, and older women too, ladies who looked rather too homely, mothers like me probably, but mothers with kids, with irrecoverable waistlines, all wearing rather short skirts and high heels and tight sweaters, like me, badly made up, it was absurd really, if we appeared at all, it would be naked. Some had brought their children, who were running up and down the stairs, the other women clowned around with them when they passed. There were a lot of students there too, in jeans and T-shirts, they would have parents, what would their parents think if their daughters were chosen and they happened to see the film one day; even if it was only going to be sold on video, they do what they like with them after that, they end up being shown on television in the small hours of the morning, and an insomniac father is capable of anything, a mother less so. People are really hard-up and there's a lot of unemployment: they plonk themselves down in front of the television and watch anything that's on just to kill time or kill the emptiness, nothing shocks them, when you have nothing, everything seems acceptable, atrocities seem normal and any moral scruples go by the board, and, after all, this kind of filth doesn't actually do any harm, it can even be quite interesting sometimes. You can learn things.

Two men came out of the upstairs room in which they were doing the screen tests, beyond the waiting room, and when they saw the queue, they clutched their hands to their heads and decided to go through it slowly – stair by stair – thinning it out. "You can go," they said to one lady. "You're not right, you're not suitable, there's no point waiting," they said to the other matrons, as well as to the young women who looked too timid or too thick, they addressed all of them as "tú". They even asked one girl for her identity card right there and then. "I haven't got it on me," she said. "Then you can get out, we don't want any problems with under-age girls," said the taller man, who the other man called Mir. The shorter one had a moustache and seemed politer and more considerate. They reduced the queue by three quarters, so there were only eight or nine of us left and we all went in, one by one. A girl ahead of me came out a few minutes later crying, I don't know if it was because they had rejected her or because they'd made her do something humiliating. Perhaps they'd made fun of her body. But if you go in for these things, you must know what to expect. They didn't do anything to me, just the usual, they told me to take my clothes off, bit by bit at first. Sitting at a table were Mir and the short man and another guy with a ponytail, like a triumvirate, then a couple of technicians, and, standing up, a guy in red trousers, with a face like a monkey, standing there with his arms folded, I don't know what he was doing there, perhaps he was a friend who had dropped in for the session, a peeping Tom, a sex maniac, he looked like a sex maniac. They shot some video film, had a good look at me, this way and that, in the flesh and on screen, turn around, raise your arms, the usual, obviously I was a bit embarrassed, but I almost felt like laughing when I saw them jotting down notes on index cards, all very serious, as if they were teachers at an oral exam, good grief.

"You can get dressed," they said then. "Be here the day after tomorrow at ten o'clock. But make sure you get a good night's sleep, don't come back with those great dark rings under your eyes, they really show up on screen." It was Mir who said that, and it was true, I did have rings under my eyes, I'd hardly slept a wink all night, thinking about the screen test. I was just leaving when the guy with the ponytail, who the others called Custardoy, called me back. "Hey," he said, "just so there aren't any surprises

or problems and so that you don't let us down at the last minute:
you'll have to do a bit of French, a bit of Cuban and a fuck,
all right?" He turned to the tall man to confirm this: "She won't
have to do any Greek, will she?" "No, not with her, not seeing
she's a novice," said Mir. The primate uncrossed his arms and
crossed them again the other way round, annoyed, God, he
looked a sight in his red trousers. I tried to remember quickly;
I'd heard those terms, or seen them in sex ads in the paper,
perhaps I'd even known what they meant, more or less. No
Greek, they'd said, so that didn't really matter, at least for now.
French was obviously a blow job, but Cuban?

"What does Cuban mean?" I asked.

The short man looked at me disapprovingly.

"You know," he said, and he raised his hands to his non-
existent breasts. I wasn't sure I quite understood, but I only dared
ask one other question:

"Have you chosen my partner yet?" I felt like saying "my
fellow actor", but I thought they might think I was taking the
piss.

"Yes, you'll meet him the day after tomorrow. Don't worry,
he's very experienced and he'll take the lead." That was the
expression the short man used, as if he were describing a ball-
room dance, when it still made sense to say: "I'll lead."

Now I was back again in the waiting room, waiting for filming
to begin, waiting with my partner, to whom I'd just been introduced, he shook my hand. We'd sat down on the rather narrow
sofa, so small that he, at once, moved to a matching armchair in
order to be more comfortable. The tall guy and the short guy
and the one with the ponytail and the technicians were filming
with another couple (I hoped the sex maniac wouldn't be there,
he frightened me with his bulbous eyes, his flattened nose and his
hideous trousers). In films, so I've heard, everything takes for ever

and everything's always running late, and so they told us to wait
and get to know each other. That was absurd. "I don't know
this man from Adam and yet, in a few minutes from now, I'll be
sucking him off," I thought and I couldn't help thinking it in
those precise words. "What's the point of our getting to know
each other a bit and having a chat." I hardly dared look at him,
I did so out of the corner of my eye, a rather unfortunate attack
of modesty. When they introduced me to him, they had said:
"This is Loren, your partner." I would have preferred it if they'd
called him my "co-star", but I suppose that would have been a bit
pretentious. He was about thirty, he was wearing trousers and a
hat and cowboy boots, actors are always so Americanized, even if
they only appear in porn movies. That's how a lot of them start, he
might make it big one day. He wasn't at all bad-looking, despite
appearances, an athletic sort, the type that goes to the gym a lot,
he had a slightly hooked nose and grey eyes, calm and cold; he had
a nice mouth, but that wasn't perhaps what I would have to kiss,
that nice mouth. He seemed completely unfazed, he was sitting
with his legs crossed like a cowboy and was leafing through a
newspaper, he didn't take much notice of me. He had smiled at
me when we were introduced, he had gaps between his teeth
which gave his face a rather child-like look. He'd taken off his hat
then, but had immediately put it back on again, perhaps he would
keep it on during the filming. He offered me some liquorice
sweets, but I declined, he sucked two at a time, perhaps it would
be best if we didn't kiss after all. On his wrist he wore a strap made
out of leather or elephant skin, very tight. I wouldn't call it a
bracelet exactly. I suppose he looked modern, I felt suddenly very
old-fashioned in my tight skirt, my black tights and my heels, I
don't know why the hell I put on the highest heels I've got,
perhaps, if they noticed them, they'd want me to keep them on,
a lot of men like to see women like that, naked and in high heels,

it's all a bit infantile that imagery, him with his hat on and me in my high heels. I realized that I was pulling my skirt down a bit, because it had ridden up while I was sitting, and that struck me as ludicrous. Not even my co-star was taking any notice of my thighs, and he was right, in a little while, there would be no skirt, no nothing.

"Excuse me," I said then, "you've done this kind of work before, haven't you?"

He looked up from the newspaper, but didn't put it down, as if he wasn't sure he wanted to start a proper conversation, or, rather, as if he was sure that he didn't.

"Yes," he said, "but not that much, two, no, three times, a little while ago. But don't worry, you forget about the camera straight away. They told me it was your first time." I was grateful to him for putting it like that, rather than calling me a novice as tall, bald Mir had done. "Don't get embarrassed, that's fatal, just follow me and try and enjoy it as much as you can, and take no notice of the others."

"Easier said than done," I replied. "I hope they're patient if I get nervous. I am a bit nervous."

The actor Lorenzo gave me his gap-toothed smile. He was reading the sports pages. He seemed very sure of himself, because he said:

"Look, you won't even notice that they're filming. I'll take care of that." He said it more ingenuously than proudly, that wasn't what was worrying me, but it did worry me that it didn't even occur to him that it wouldn't be the people watching who would be the main cause of my nervousness on the set.

"Right," I said, not daring to doubt him, perhaps intimidated. "But there'll be breaks won't there? For the different takes and so on? And what happens then? What do you do in between?"

"Nothing, you can put on a dressing gown if you like and

have a Coca-Cola. Don't worry," he said again. "There are worse things. And there's bound to be a few lines of coke if you need it."

"Oh, so there are worse things, are there?" I said a little irritated by his excessive lack of concern. "I obviously just haven't come across them yet; go on tell me one." He finally put the newspaper down and I added hastily: "I'm not saying that because of you. I didn't mean you, you do understand that, don't you? I'm just doing it for the money, but you're not going to tell me that it's still not a pretty awful thing to have to do. Well, I don't know about you, but it is for me."

Loren ignored my attempts not to offend him and focused on what I had said before. He looked at me with his calm eyes, but he seemed slightly irritated now, as if he had been provoked and as if he were someone who had no capacity for feeling provoked, and didn't know what tone of voice to use. His grey eyes were slightly wide-set too, quite far from his hooked nose, that seemed to draw his lips upwards, the kind of nostrils that always look as if their owner has a cold.

"There is something worse," he said. "And I'm going to tell you about it now. What I used to do before was much worse, not that I'm going to do this for ever, but it's all right to be going on with until something else turns up, and you have no idea how great it is compared with what I used to do before."

"What did you used to do, then? Did someone throw knives at you in a circus?"

I don't know why I said that. I suppose it must have sounded offensive as if the actor Lorenzo must, inevitably, have come from the lowest sphere of the entertainment world. After all, I was only doing what he was doing, and I'd merely lost my job two years ago and had an ex-husband who had disappeared, gone missing, and a daughter to look after. He probably had a daughter too. And besides, they don't have shows like that now, that's old hat, there aren't even many circuses any more.

"Look, smartypants," he said, but without sounding in the least reproachful and without intending to wound me, I'm not sure if that was simply because he was very tolerant or because he didn't know how to. He said it the way children say it at school: "No, smartypants. I was a guardian."

"A guardian? What do you mean a 'guardian'? A guardian of what?" That was the last word I'd expected to hear from his lips and I couldn't conceal my surprise, which may have seemed offensive. I looked him full in the face, a guardian, he looked more like someone out of a spaghetti western.

He touched the brim of his hat uneasily, as if straightening it.

"Well, I mean, I had someone under my guardianship, under my protection. Like being a bodyguard, only different."

"Oh, a bodyguard," I said, pulling a face, as if placing him further down the hierarchy. "And what was so bad about that? Were you constantly having to come between your boss and the bullets or something?" I had no reason to get stroppy with him, but I just kept coming out with these impertinent replies, perhaps I was beginning to feel sickened by the idea of soon having to suck him off with no preliminaries, time was moving on. Involuntarily I looked at his crotch, and immediately looked away again. I thought it again using that verb, 'suck him off', this modern age is making us all foul-mouthed, or perhaps we don't much care if we are, or perhaps it's just poverty: the less money you have, the fewer scruples too. And the older we get, the less life there is, there's not that long left.

"No, I wasn't that kind of bodyguard, I'm not a goon," he said, not at all put out by my sarcasm, but speaking seriously, frankly, transparently. "I had to keep watch over a person who was ill, to stop her harming herself, it's very difficult. You have to watch them twenty-four hours a day, be alert all the time and you can't always manage it."

"Who was she? What happened to her?"

Loren took off his hat and stroked the top of it with his right forearm, the way cowboys do in films. Perhaps it was a gesture of respect. His hair was thinning.

"She was the daughter of a rich guy, a multimillionaire, unbelievable, one of those businessmen who doesn't even know how much money he's got. You'd know his name, but I'd best not tell you. The daughter was crazy, a hysteric with suicidal tendencies, every so often she'd try and kill herself. For weeks at a time, she would lead an apparently normal life and then, suddenly, with no prior warning, she'd slit her wrists in the bath. She was completely nuts. They didn't want to hospitalize her because that would be too cruel and because the whole world and his wife would end up finding out about it, whereas only a few people, the people who were close to her, knew about the suicide attempts. So they took me on in order to stop it happening, so, yes, I was a bodyguard but not to protect her from others, as a bodyguard would normally do, but to protect her from herself. Her friends took me for a normal bodyguard, but I wasn't. My job was different, it was more like being a custodian."

I thought that he probably knew that word because he had taken the trouble to find one that would describe his role. He would have recognized it when he found it.

"I see," I said. "And that was worse than this. How old was she? Why didn't they get a nurse to look after her?"

Loren passed the back of his hand under his chin, against the grain, as if he had suddenly realized he wasn't properly shaven. He was going to have to kiss me everywhere. But he seemed well-shaven enough to me, I was tempted to touch his face myself, but I didn't dare, he might have taken it for a caress.

"For the same reason, because a nurse is more obvious, what's a young girl doing all day with a nurse hanging around? You could understand her having a bodyguard, with her super-rich Daddy. She could lead a normal life, you see, she was going to university, she was twenty years old, she went to parties and to other flash dos, to the psychiatrist as well, of course, but it wasn't like she was depressed all day or anything, no. She'd be normal for a while, and friendly. Suddenly she'd get an attack and it was always a suicidal one, and you could never tell when it would happen. There were no sharp objects in her bedroom, no scissors, no penknives, nothing, no belts she could hang herself with, no tablets anywhere, not even aspirin; not even high-heeled shoes, her mother was always careful to make sure they weren't too sharp ever since the time her daughter slashed her own cheekbone with one, they had to give her plastic surgery, you couldn't tell, but she'd given herself a really nasty gash. She wouldn't have been allowed to wear the shoes you've got on, quite a weapon really. In that sense, they treated her like a prisoner, no dangerous objects allowed. Her father was almost on the point of taking away her sunglasses when he saw *Godfather III*, in which someone kills another man with his glasses, with the sharp part of the arm, honestly, they'd given the guy a full body search and he goes and cuts the other guy's throat with that. Have you seen *Godfather III*?"

"No I haven't. I saw the first one."

"If you like, I can lend you the video," said Loren amiably. "It's by far the best of the three."

"I haven't got a video. Go on," I said, fearing that at any moment the door would open to reveal the tall face of Mir or the bony face of Custardoy or the short man's moustache, in order for us to start filming our scenes. We wouldn't be able to talk during them, not in the same way, we'd have to concentrate, get on with it.

"Anyway, I had to be around her all day and sleep with one eye open, I had the room next to hers, her room and mine were joined by a connecting door to which I had the key, you know, like you get in hotels sometimes, the house was enormous. But, of course, there are countless ways you can hurt yourself, if someone really wants to kill themselves, they'll do it in the end, just like a murderer, if someone wants to kill someone, they'll end up doing it however well protected their victim is, even if it's the Prime Minister, even if it's the King, if someone is determined to kill and they don't care about the consequences, they'll kill whoever they like, there's nothing you can do about it, they've got nothing to lose if they don't care what happens afterwards. Look at Kennedy, look at India, there's hardly a politician left alive there. Well, it's the same thing with someone who wants to murder herself, attempted suicides just make me laugh. The princess would throw herself headfirst down the escalator in a big department store and we'd pick her up with a great gash in her forehead and her legs all grazed, it was just lucky I was there. Or she'd hurl herself against a display cabinet, against a shop window in the middle of the street, you've no idea what that's like, covered in cuts and with hundreds of glass splinters stuck in her, absolute madness, and howling with pain, because if you don't manage to kill yourself, it really hurts. They couldn't lock her up either, that wouldn't have cured her. I got used to seeing danger everywhere, that's the real horror, seeing the whole world as a threat, nothing is innocent and everything is against you, I saw enemies in the most inoffensive things, my imagination had to anticipate hers, I had to grab her arm every time we were going to cross the street, make sure she didn't go near any high windows, be very careful in swimming pools, move her out of the path of any workman walking past carrying a pole because she might try and impale herself on it, well, that's how I came to see things, she was capable of anything, you start to distrust everything, people, objects, walls." – "That's how I used to be when my daughter was small," I thought, "I'm still a bit like that even now, I'm never completely at ease. I know what that's like. Yes, it is horrible." – "Once, she tried to throw herself under the horses' hooves in the final straight at the races, luckily, I managed to grab her by the ankle when she was just about to step onto the track, she took advantage of the fact that I was placing the bets and she slipped away from me, God, the panic I went through until I found her, she was already running towards the horses." The actor Lorenzo made only a verbal pause, not a mental one, I could see that he was still thinking about what he was telling or going to tell. "I can assure you, that was much worse than this, terrible tension, constant anxiety, especially after I'd fucked her, I fucked her twice: well, connecting door, me having the key, the nights spent always half-awake and jumpy, it was sort of inevitable. Besides, whilst I was there with her there was no danger, nothing could happen to her while I was on top of her with my arms around her, with me on top of her she was safe, you see." – "Sex is the safest place," I thought, "you control the other person, you keep them immobilized and safe." It had been a long time since I'd been in that safe place. – "But of course, you screw a woman a couple of times and you get fond of her. Well, not that fond, I've got a girlfriend too, and not because you have to, but it's different, you've touched her, you've kissed her and you don't look at her the same any more, and she treats you affectionately too." I wondered if I would treat him affectionately after the session awaiting us. Or if he would get fond of me because of that. I didn't interrupt. "So apart from the tension involved in the work, there was also the worry, not to say panic, I didn't want anything to happen to her, that was the last thing in the world I wanted. In short, it was a real bummer; beside that, this is a breeze."

"Bummer" and "breeze", you hear those words less and less, they sounded almost funny.

"Yes," I said. "What happened, did you get fed up?" I asked, not expecting him to answer in the affirmative. In fact, he'd already told me what had happened, by the way he stopped to think before telling me the rest.

Loren put his hat back on and breathed hard out of those damp nostrils, as if he were gathering strength before doing something that required an effort. The brim of his hat covered his cold, grey eyes, his face was now just nose and lips, the nice lips that I would not kiss, there are no kisses on the mouth in porn movies.

"No, I lost my job. I failed. The princess slit her throat in the kitchen of her house three weeks ago, in the middle of the night, and I didn't even hear her leave the bedroom, what do you think of that? I was left with no one to look after. A disaster, a complete disaster." For a moment, I was seized by the thought that perhaps the actor Lorenzo was just acting in order to distract me and ease my nerves. I thought for a moment about my little girl, I'd left her with a neighbour. He stood up, paced round the room, at the same time hitching up his jeans. He stopped by the closed door through which we would soon have to pass. I thought he was going to punch it, but he didn't. He just said irritably: "When are we going to bloody well get started, I haven't got all day."

BLOOD ON A SPEAR

For Luis Antonio de Villena

I SAID GOODBYE for ever to my best friend without knowing that I was, because the following night, after far too long a delay, he was found lying on his bed with a spear through his chest and with a strange woman by his side, also dead, but without the murder weapon impaled in her body, because the weapon was one and the same and they must have first stuck it in her, then pulled it out again in order to mingle her blood with that of my best friend. The lights were all on and the television too, and had doubtless remained so for the whole of that day, my friend's first day without life or the world's first day without his worldly presence in it after thirty-nine years, the light bulbs incongruous in the harsh morning sun and perhaps less so against the stormy afternoon sky, but Dorta would have hated all that waste. I don't quite know who pays the bills for the dead.

He had a great bulge on his head from an earlier blow, it wasn't just a swelling or, if it was, it encompassed the whole of his forehead, the skin tight over his elephantiasic cranium, as if he had become Frankensteinized in death, a small bald spot on his hairline that hadn't been there before. That blow must have knocked him out, but it would seem that he didn't entirely lose consciousness, because his eyes were open and he had his glasses on, although the man who had then stuck the spear in him might have put them on afterwards, as a joke, you don't need glasses when you know for certain that you're never going to see ever again: here you are, four-eyes, maybe these will help you find the road to hell more easily. He was wearing the bathrobe he always used as a dressing gown, he bought a new one every few months and this latest one was yellow, he should have avoided that colour, as bullfighters do. He had his slippers on, the rigid, hard-soled variety that Americans wear, a kind of moccasin cut low on the instep, with no embellishments and with a very flat heel, you feel safer if you can hear your own footsteps. His two bare legs emerged from amongst the folds of his bathrobe, and, although he was a hairy man, I saw that his shins were hairless, some people do lose the hair on their legs there from the constant rubbing of their trousers, or from their socks if they wear long socks, sports socks they call them, and he always wore them, I never once saw a strip of bare skin when he crossed his legs in public. Enough blood had flowed for enough hours – with the lights on and busy witnesses on the TV screen – to soak the bathrobe and the sheets and to ruin the wooden floor. The bed, with no bedspread on it because of the heat, had not been disturbed, the sheets hadn't been turned down. He appeared pale in the photos, as all corpses do, with an unusual expression on his face, because he was a jolly man, always laughing and joking, and his face seemed serious, rather than terrorstruck or stupefied, with a look of bitterness, or perhaps – more surprising still – mere displeasure or annoyance, as if he had been obliged to do something not particularly momentous, but against his inclinations. Since dying always seems momentous to the person if he knows that he's

dying, one could not discount the possibility that they had
stuck the spear in him while he was still stunned from the
previous blow, so he wouldn't have been aware of what was
happening, and that might explain why he didn't react when
they plunged the weapon into the breast of the unknown woman
and pulled it out again. The spear was his, brought back some
years ago as a souvenir from a trip to Kenya which he had
hated and from which he had returned complaining, as he usually
did from trips abroad. I'd often seen it, planted nonchalantly
in the umbrella stand, Dorta had always intended to hang it up
somewhere, one of those ornaments that catch your fancy
when you see it in someone else's hands and which you like
rather less when you get it home. Dorta didn't collect such
objects, but, from time to time, he gave in to a capricious
impulse, especially in countries he knew he would never go back
to. Those who disliked him saw a certain irony in the manner
of his death, for he was very keen on pointed, metal walking
sticks, of which he had quite a few. Not very original, rather
pedantic.

The woman was almost naked, wearing just a pair of knickers,
there was no trace in the house of any other items of the clothing
she must have arrived in, as if the spear-thrower had scrupulously
gathered them up after the murders and taken them away
with him, nobody walks down the street or travels in a taxi
like that, however hot it is, I mean not naked like that. Perhaps
that was a joke too: I'm going to leave you there naked, you
whore, that way you can go on being screwed all the way to
hell. An unnecessary hassle for a murderer in any case, everything
that remains accuses, everything that remains on our hands. The
woman was about thirty, judging by her appearance and by the
forensic report, and, judging by her appearance alone, she could
have been an immigrant, Cuban or Dominican or Guatemalan,

for example, she had bronzed skin, full, slightly cracked lips and prominent cheekbones, but there are a lot of Spanish women like that too, in the south and in the centre and even in the north, not to mention the islands, people are less easy to classify than we might think. She had her eyes closed and an expression of pain on her face, as if she hadn't died immediately and had had time to make that involuntary gesture, the agony of the iron entering her flesh and having entered her flesh, her teeth instinctively clenching and her vision clouding, her nakedness experienced suddenly as a kind of extra defencelessness, it's different if a sharp weapon first has to penetrate fabric, however fine, than if it pierces the skin directly, although the results are identical. That's what I think anyway, not that I've ever been injured in that way, touch wood, fingers crossed. The woman was wounded beneath her left breast, both of which looked soft, as far as I could make out and given that I was looking at them for the first time in photos, hardly ideal. But you get used to imagining the texture and volume and feel of women the first time you see them, especially in these deceitful times, if she'd been rich she would have had silicon implants, especially at her age, a kind of consubstantial softness impervious to passing time. Her breasts were smeared with dried blood. She had long, tangled, curly hair, and part of her hair covered her right cheek in a rather unnatural fashion, as if she had had time to pull her hair over her face in an attempt to cover it, a final gesture of modesty or shame regarding her anonymous posterity. In a way, I felt sorry for her, I had the feeling that her death was secondary, that it wasn't really to do with her or that she was only part of the decor. She had some semen in her mouth and, according to the report, the semen belonged to Dorta. It also said that some of her teeth were decayed, the teeth of a poor woman, or the victims of sweets. It also said that substances were found in both organisms, that was the word, "substances", what exactly it didn't say, though I don't find it particularly hard to imagine.

Both were in a seated position, or rather they weren't lying down, but reclining, although in the case of my friend I was not spared one particularly unpleasant detail: the rusty spear had penetrated him with such force that the point, never honed or polished or even cleaned since it arrived from Kenya – but extremely sharp – had gone straight through his chest into the wall, leaving him pinned to the plaster like an insect. If someone had told Dorta about this, he would have shuddered to think of the plaster left inside the body when the spear was removed, someone had to take it out, it would undoubtedly have required more force than that used by the person who had impaled it in the two chests, one female, one male. The weapon had not been thrown from any distance, it had been thrust in from below, possibly at a run, possibly not, but if not, the person holding it must have been either very strong or accustomed to bayonetting. It was a large bedroom, there was enough space to take a run-up, the whole of Dorta's apartment was very large, an old apartment that had been renovated, a legacy from his parents, he only bothered about two areas, the living room and the bedroom, the place was too big for him. He had just turned thirty-nine, he bemoaned the fact that his fortieth birthday was just around the corner, he lived alone, but often invited people round, one at a time.

"The worst thing about ages is that they always seem so alien," he said to me the night of his death, during supper. His birthday had been a week before, but I hadn't been able to celebrate it with him then because he'd been away in London that day. I hadn't been able to make the traditional jokes, I was three months younger than him and, during those three months, I used to call him "granddad". Now I'm two years older than he will ever be, I've turned the corner. "A few days ago, I read a newspaper article about a man of thirty-seven, and, in fact, the association of that age and the word 'man' seemed quite appropriate, at least for that individual. For me, on the other hand, it wouldn't. I still unconsciously expect people to refer to me as 'a young man', and, of course, I expect them to call me 'tú', yet I'm two years older than the man in the article. I think only other people should have birthdays. No, I'd go further, just as in the past the rich would pay a poor person to do their military service or to go to war instead of them, it should be possible to engage someone to have our birthdays for us. Every now and then, we would have one ourselves, this year is mine, I'm bored with being thirty-nine. Don't you think that would be an excellent idea?"

It would never have occurred to either of us that, in his case, thirty-nine would be the fixed number with which he could bore himself until the end of time with absolutely no possibility of changing it. That was the kind of idea Dorta came up with when he was in good spirits and in a good mood, rather silly, mad ideas, a bit daft and invariably puerile, which was quite justified, at least with me, because we'd known each other since we were children and it's hard not to continue to behave with a person the way you would have behaved when you first met: if you were a bit of a fusspot, then, from time to time, you should continue to be so; if you were cruel, if you were frivolous, if you were enigmatic, shifty, weak or beloved, we have a different repertoire for each person, the contents of which we are allowed to vary but not relinquish, if someone laughed once they will always have to laugh, otherwise, they will be rejected. And that is why I always called Dorta "Dorta" and that is how I remember him, at school you were known by your surname until you reached adolescence. And just as when you stay in touch with someone, you continue to see superimposed on their adult face the face of the child with whom you once shared a desk, as if any later changes or any accentuation of certain features were a mask and a game intended to conceal the essence, so the achievements or failures of the various ages of the other person seem unreal or rather fictitious, like the plans or fantasies or imaginings or fears with which childhood is peopled, as if between those friends whatever happened still seemed to be and was still experienced as a hope – the primary childhood state of mind is not even desire – the present as well as the past and even the distant past. With such friends very little can be taken absolutely seriously because you're used to everything being pretend, introduced explicitly by those formulae that you later abandon when you go out into the world, "Let's play at . . . ," "Let's pretend that . . . ," "I'm the leader now" (you only abandon them verbally, in reality it all goes on the same). That's why I can talk of his death dispassionately, as if it were something that had not yet happened, but was part of the eternal waiting for all that is unlikely and impossible. "Imagine someone killed me with a spear." A spear, in Madrid. But sometimes passion surfaces – or possibly rage – for just those reasons, because I can imagine the anguish and panic that night of a person I still see as a nervous, resigned child whom I often had to defend in the playground, and who would later apologize and give me a book or a comic because he'd forced me to get into a fight with the heavies when there was no need for me to do so – not that he ever asked for my help, he just let himself be punched or pushed around, that's all; but I saw it – to waste my energies on someone who could never win in a physical fight and whose glasses ended up on the ground almost every day of every school year. It's unforgivable that he should have died a violent death, even though he never knew what happened. But that's pure rhetoric, who doesn't know when they're dying? I wasn't there to see him and to go into battle for him, although it was a near thing.

His stay in London had coincided with an auction at Sotheby's of literary and historical items which some diplomatic friends had encouraged him to attend. They were selling all kinds of documents and objects that had belonged to writers and politicians. Letters, postcards, billets-doux, telegrams, whole manuscripts, rough drafts, files, photos, a lock of Byron's hair, the long pipe that Peter Cushing smoked in *The Hound of the Baskervilles*, Churchill's cigar butts, engraved cigarette cases, over-elaborate walking sticks, tried and tested amulets. It wasn't an unusual walking stick that had aroused his capricious buyer's impulse during the bidding, but a ring that had belonged to Crowley, Aleister Crowley, he explained benevolently, a medi-ocre writer and a self-declared madman who called himself "The Great Beast" and "The wickedest man in the world", all his private possessions had 666 engraved on them, the number of the Beast according to the Apocalypse, nowadays rock groups with demonic pretensions play around with the number, but it's also to be found hidden in many computers, it's the joker's number, the living have no idea how old everything is, remarked Dorta, how hard it is to be new, what do young people know about Crowley, the orgiast and satanist, he'd probably be considered a harmless, naive conservative these days, a kindly man at heart who transformed his disciple Victor Neuburg into a zebra for making too many mistakes during an invocation of the Devil in the Sahara, so Dorta told me, and rode on his back all the way to Alexandria, where he sold him to a zoo which looked after the incompetent disciple or, rather, zebra for two years, until Crowley finally allowed him to resume his human form, he was a compassionate man at heart. Neuburg later became a publisher.

"A magic ring, that's how it was described in the catalogue, with a precious oval emerald set in platinum with the inscription 'Iaspar Balthazar Melcior', I wasn't sure the ring would fit, but even so I bid like a mad thing, way above my limit." Dorta had told me all this while his good mood lasted, when he was happy he would talk endlessly, then he would grow quiet and ask about me and my life, he would let me be the one to do the talking, two consecutive monologues rather than a real dialogue. "The other bidders gradually fell away apart from one guy with a Germanic face and one of those noses that always looks as if it must have a dewdrop hanging from it, it made me feel like passing him a handkerchief and banishing him to a corner, a tapir's nose, a guy with irritating features, he was well dressed, but he was wearing crocodile-skin cowboy boots, you can imagine the effect, the mere sight of them was enough to enrage you. I bid higher and he bid higher, steadily and without moving a muscle, merely lifting his nose as if he were a mechanical toy, I looked at him out of the corner of my eye each time I increased my bid and saw the apparently bedewdropped nose rising up like the little flag on ancient traffic lights, or was it taxis that used to have those? anyway, he blocked my way each time, forcing me to make rapid mental conversions from sterling into pesetas only to realize that I was offering a sum of money that I didn't actually possess."

"Really? The magic ring couldn't have been that expensive, Dorta," I said mockingly. He didn't have much money, but he pretended he did, he behaved like a spendthrift and he rarely deprived himself of anything he fancied, at least not with witnesses present, meanness was a blight. Of course, the things he fancied were never excessive, they didn't require a large outlay, as people used to say, or so I thought, I don't know how much everything cost. Anyway, he had enough to pay for his vital pleasures.

"Well, yes, I could have gone a bit higher, but that would have meant making small sacrifices later on, which are the kind I hate most, it's the small sacrifices that make you feel really miserable. And it's so much harder to give things up in the summer. Anyway, the other man kept raising his nose again and again, like some malfunctioning level crossing, until one of my companions grabbed me by the elbow and stopped me putting my hand up.'You can't afford it, Eugenio, you'll regret it,' he whispered, and I really don't know why he whispered, no one there understood Spanish. But he was right and I didn't pull away and I felt wretched, I immediately fell into a great depression, I'm still in it, and I had to put up with seeing that dripping nose lift once more and look at me defiantly, as if saying: 'I beat you, what did you expect?' He left at once, clattering out in his crocodile-skin cowboy boots, he didn't stay for the rest of the auction, although he may have come back later for other lots, I don't know, because I too left after a couple more bids. It was a terrible humiliation, Víctor, and it happened abroad of all places."

He called me Víctor, not by my surname, Francés, as he usually did. He only called me Víctor when he was feeling under the weather or he felt alone. I never called him Eugenio, ever. Dorta still had a lot of Dorta the little boy in him, but also a great deal of his mother and his aunts whom I had often seen on the way out of school or in their various homes, invited there by their son or nephew. From time to time, he came out with some phrase that doubtless belonged to those innocent, antiquated ladies who had so dominated his world. He just came out with them, he didn't avoid them, indeed, he probably enjoyed perpetuating those ladies like that, verbally, through their lost turns-of-phrase: "and it happened abroad of all places".

"What the hell did you want the ring for anyway?" I asked. "You haven't started believing in magic I hope. Or was there someone you wanted to transform into a giraffe?"

"No, don't worry. It just took my fancy, it amused me, it was unusual and it had a history behind it, if I'd worn it here lots of people would have asked me about it, it's all grist to the mill when you're trying to chat someone up in a bar. The only magic I believe in is other people's, not my own, of course; I've never been touched by magic once in my entire life, as you well know." And he added smiling: "In fact, when I lost the ring, I regretted not having bid for the previous lot on your behalf, it wasn't that expensive. 'Crowley's magic talisman for sexual potency and power over women,' was how it was described in the catalogue, what do you think, a nice silver medallion with the inevitable 666 engraved on it. The German or whatever he was made off with that too, only he wasn't competing with me for that one, perhaps that's why it was less expensive. At least I have the consolation of knowing that I forced him to pay far too much money for the ring. What do you think: 'power over women'? It was engraved with the initials AC as well as the number. You might have found it useful."

I laughed at his malice which, when directed at me, was always benign, not necessarily with others, though, his tongue was his only weapon.

"I'm sure it would have been in a few years' time, I can see it now. But at the moment, I haven't much to complain about in either respect."

"Oh really? Tell me all about it."

Perhaps that was the moment when I started talking during our last supper together and he listened with interest, but seemed slightly cast down too; if he fell silent for too long, that usually meant he was worried about something or momentarily dissatisfied with himself or with his life, it happens to all of us from time to time, but it doesn't last if there are no serious grounds for it, concern about the uncertain future or about every-day regrets, for which there isn't much time, genuine regret requires both perdurability and time. When a friend dies we want to remember everything about the last occasion we saw them, the supper that we experienced as just another supper, but which suddenly acquires unmerited significance and insists on shining with a light not its own; we try to see meaning where there was none, we try to see signs and indications and perhaps magic. If the friend has died a violent death what we try to see are perhaps clues, without realizing that something might equally well not have happened that night, and then the clues would be false ones. I remember that, after supper, he was happily smoking some Indonesian cigarettes that he'd brought back from London and that tasted and smelled of cloves. He gave me a packet which I still have, it's a brand called Gudang Garam, a slim red packet, "12 kretek cigarettes", I don't know what "kretek" means, it must be an Indonesian word. The health warning doesn't beat about the bush, it says bluntly "Smoking kills". Of course it didn't kill Dorta, he was killed by an African spear. When I stopped regaling him with my anodyne tales, he again took over the talk with renewed energy having returned from the bathroom, but he was no longer cheerful. With one forefinger he traced the little relief design on the box, it looked like a stretch of railway track, forming a curve, a railway landscape, to the left there were some childish houses with triangular roofs, perhaps a station, all in black, gold and red.

"I don't think I'm going to have a very good time this summer," he said. It was already the end of July, later, I thought how odd that he should think he had the whole summer still lying ahead of him that night. "It's going to be difficult for me,

I'm a bit crazy at the moment, and the worst thing is that the things I always used to enjoy now bore me. Even writing bores me." He paused and added with a feeble smile, as if he had committed some impropriety: "My last book was a complete flop, much worse than you might imagine. I'm finishing something else as quickly as I can, you mustn't give failures time to stew, because they immediately impregnate and contaminate everything, every aspect of your existence, however remote, however removed it might be from the area where the disaster occurred, like a bloodstain. Although, of course, you then run the risk of having two failures on the trot and end up getting even more besmirched. Some people go under precisely because of that. Tonight I'm meeting the publisher who's signed a contract for my current book, even though I haven't finished it. I've arranged to have a drink with him, he's on a brief visit to Madrid and wants me to entertain him. He's a man entirely without scruples and he talks really slowly, an utter bore. But he doesn't know what I'm like yet and he enjoyed luring me away from the others. Well, the way things are, 'luring' is just a manner of speaking. Soon I won't even be a name, what people call 'a name that rings a bell', a known author."

His nights only really began after supper. After the publisher would come the real fun, open-air cafés and discotheques and wandering around with other people until dawn or thereabouts, it wasn't so very odd that he should still have expected to be regarded as a young man. The truth is he looked older, I suppose, I find it hard to say, but people who knew us both were surprised to find we had been classmates, and it's not that I look particularly young for my age. He seemed worried, pessimistic, insecure, perhaps weighed down by the recent discovery that even something that takes a long time to come about may still not last, relative success in his case, which should have continued but instead came to a halt, all too soon, allowing him only a brief taste of the good life. I prefer not to comment on his novels, two years on no one reads them any more, the author is no longer in the world to defend them and to continue evolving, although his violent death meant that the posthumous, unfinished work sold wildly at first, he made the non-literary headlines for a few weeks, and the unscrupulous publisher rushed the book out. I had no desire to read it by then.

After a while, there were no more headlines, no more small print, nothing, Dorta was immediately forgotten, his books worthless apart from their curiosity value, his murder unresolved and therefore abandoned, anything that does not advance or continue to evolve is condemned to a very rapid dissolution. The police either closed the file or not, I don't know quite how their bureaucracy works, but, from the very first, they didn't seem to me to have much interest in finding out anything – they're lazy people, the day of judgement is a long way off – once they knew that the strangest and most mysterious element had a simple explanation, the souvenir spear. However, the strangest or most mysterious element was not the spear, but the unknown woman by his side with his semen on her gums, because Dorta was homosexual – how can I put it – unwaveringly homosexual, and, looking back, I suppose he had been from that first day in the playground and in class, although neither he nor I, neither then nor for many years afterwards, knew the word existed nor what it meant. Perhaps the school bullies knew or, rather, guessed, which is why they were so horrible to him. I would go so far as to say that he had never been with a woman in his life, apart from the odd perverse snog in adolescence, when nonconformity is a very serious matter if you don't want to be isolated, and when everyone is trying so hard both to attract attention and at the same time to be part of the group. His nights were often spent

searching, but it wasn't women he was chatting up in those bars
where anything was grist to the mill. He wasn't horny enough
to make exceptions or to feel flattered if some woman came on to
him or made him an offer, which was most unlikely, women can
sense desire in a man, however sluggish and lukewarm, and no
woman would ever have sensed any desire in him. That was the
most peculiar thing about his death, more even than the violence,
for he had been a victim of minor violence on a few previous
occasions, I suppose going to bed with strange men who are
always stronger and younger and poorer than yourself does have
its risks. He never told me whether or not he paid for sex and I
never asked, perhaps he had to as – much to his bemusement – he
became "a man". I know that he gave them presents and indulged
their every whim according to his means and his enthusiasm, a
less crude way of buying someone than with actual money,
rather old-fashioned really, respectable, courteous, and one that
would have allowed him to deceive himself for a while. If he
had been found lying next to a boy, it would all have seemed
much less strange to me, to the extent – a very limited extent –
that the death of anyone who has always been a part of our
lives can be considered not to be strange. Not even the age of
the Dominican/Cuban woman reflected his preferences, even
a *man* of that age would have had little interest for Dorta, too
old. I hesitated for a moment about whether I should say
anything to the inspector who questioned me and showed me
those posthumous photos. Dorta had been careful while his
mother was alive, and was still fairly careful as long as his aunts
were alive too, not that they ever knew anything about it;
nothing was made explicit in his books, there were only hints. I
think I hesitated about telling the inspector out of some sort of
absurd masculine pride: perhaps it was no bad thing that he
should believe that my best friend had spent his last night with

a woman out of choice and habit, as if that were somehow more dignified or praiseworthy. I immediately felt ashamed of that temptation, I even thought that the woman might simply be another form of mockery, like the glasses: your cum in a woman's mouth for all eternity, you filthy queer. And so I told the inspector of this remarkable circumstance, about that whole inexplicable scene, Dorta in bed with a woman, the remains of his semen in the interstices of her decaying teeth or in the lines and cracks of her full lips. But the inspector looked at me reproachfully, sarcastically, as if I had suddenly been revealed to him as a bad friend or some kind of loony wanting to muddy Dorta's memory with these wild tales when Dorta was no longer there to defend himself or to say that I was wrong, Inspector Gómez Alday shared my masculine pride, except that he made no attempt to hide his.

"Really," I insisted when I saw his look, "my friend never once went with a woman in his entire life."

"Well, he obviously decided to go with one at his death, he nearly left it too late to try," he replied in a bad-tempered, dismissive tone. He lit each cigarette, low in tar and nicotine, with the butt of the previous one. "Just what are you trying to tell me? I find a guy who's been skewered by the husband or pimp of the wife or whore he took home with him to suck him off, and you tell me he was a fairy. Come on," he said.

"Is that how you explain it? A husband or a pimp? And why the hell would a pimp do that?"

"You don't know, eh, well, you don't know much, then. Anyone can go a little crazy sometimes. They send their women off and then go mad thinking about what they'll be doing with the client. And then they lash out and kill someone, some of them are very sentimental, I can tell you. It seems like an open-and-shut case to me, so don't come to me with these stories of yours, there wasn't even anything stolen, apart from her clothes, he was obviously a bit of a fetishist this pimp. The only thing we don't know is who the stupid woman was, and we probably never will. No papers, no clothes, she looks like a Latino to me, there's probably no record of her anywhere, the only one who'll know anything about her is the one who speared her."

"I'm telling you that there's no way my friend would have picked up a tart." The police are always intimidating, we end up talking to them the way they talk to us in order to ingratiate ourselves, and they talk like members of the underworld.

"Do you want to make work for me? Do you want me to have to go into those gay dives where men slow-dance together, and get my bum felt up, when the woman involved is nothing but a whore? Come off it. I'm not going to lose time or sleep over that. If your friend really did only fancy men, then you tell me what happened. And even if he did fancy men, on the night in question he obviously decided to get himself a whore, there can't be much doubt about that, sheer chance, most unfortunate. I couldn't give a damn what he did on every other night of his life, he could have been screwing his own grandfather for all I care." Now it was my turn to look at him reproachfully, but not in the least sarcastically. He might have to deal with things like that every day, but I didn't, and it was my best friend he was talking about. He was a tall, rather burly man with receding hair and somnolent eyes which, from time to time, seemed to wake up as if in the middle of a bad dream, flashing into sudden life before returning to their apparent sleepy state. He understood and added in a more patient, conciliatory tone: "Go on, then, you tell me what you think happened, give me your version of events."

"I don't know," I said, defeated. "But, as I said, it looks like a set-up to me. You should check it out, it's your job."

Inspector Gómez Alday duly questioned the unscrupulous

publisher with whom Dorta had had a drink in Chicote, he had turned up there with his wife, the three of them left at about two in the morning and went their separate ways. The waiters, who knew Dorta by sight and by name, confirmed the time. They bumped into another friend of mine, though only an acquaintance of Dorta's, who goes by the name of Ruibérriz de Torres, but he had only stopped to talk with them for five minutes at most, until the two women he was waiting for arrived. He saw them leave at about two o'clock as well, by the revolving doors, he waved to them, he said the publisher was a dimwit but that the wife was very nice, Dorta had hardly said a word, which was odd. The couple caught a taxi in Gran Vía and went back to their hotel, they admitted feeling alarmed when Dorta said that he would walk, he told them he was going on to somewhere else nearby, and they watched as he headed off up the street towards the Telefónica or Callao, along streets rife with a fauna that terrified them, being from Barcelona, they wouldn't have walked half a block. There wasn't a breath of wind.

At the hotel, just a routine enquiry, they confirmed the arrival time of the publisher and his wife, around a quarter past two: a bit ridiculous really, the publisher may have been unscrupulous, but he would never have gone that far. Dorta was killed between five and six, as was his last, unlikely pick-up. Independently, I asked the few friends of Dorta whom I knew slightly, friends he went partying with and friends from gay bars, none of them had met up with him that night in any of his usual hang-outs, "le tour en rose" as he used to call it. They in turn asked waiters who worked in the various bars, no one had seen him, and it did seem odd that he hadn't been to any of those places that night. Perhaps it had been a special night in all respects. Perhaps he had unexpectedly got entangled with some different people who hung out in different places. Perhaps they had kidnapped him and forced him to go with his kidnappers to his apartment. But they hadn't taken anything, although someone had made off with the woman's clothes, and she perhaps was one of the gang. The spear-thrower. I didn't know what to think and so I thought absurd things. Perhaps Gómez Alday was right, perhaps he had decided to pick up an inexperienced, desperate whore, an immigrant in need of money, with a husband who wouldn't approve and would be suspicious. A question of bad luck, very bad luck.

The inspector showed me the photos which I merely glanced at. Apart from those showing the whole scene, there were a couple of close-ups of each corpse, what in the cinema is known as a close-medium shot. The woman's breasts were definitively soft, shapely and provocative, but nonetheless soft, sight and touch become fused in the end, we men sometimes look at something as if we were touching it, and this can sometimes cause offence. Despite the screwed-up eyes and the look of pain you could see that she was pretty, although you can never be sure with a naked woman, you have to see her dressed as well, beaches are of little use in that respect. Her nostrils were flared, she had a small round chin and a long neck. I glanced only quickly at the six or seven photos, but I nevertheless asked Gómez Alday if I could have a copy of the close-up of the woman; he gave me a surprised, distrustful look, as if he had uncovered some abnormality in me.

"Why do you want it?"

"I don't know," I said, lost. And I really didn't, it wasn't that I wanted to study it any further just then, a blood-stained body, a wound, the thick eyelashes, the pained expression, the soft, dead breasts, it was hardly a pleasant sight. But I thought I would like to have it perhaps in order to look at it later, in a few years' time, after all, apart from the murderer, she was the last person to have seen Dorta alive. And she had seen him at very close quarters. "It interests me." It was a feeble, not to say, grotesque argument.

Gómez Alday gave me one of his scorching looks, it didn't last long, his eyes immediately resumed their usual sleepy appearance. I thought he must be thinking that I was a man with macabre tastes, sick in the head, but perhaps he understood both my request and the desire, we did, after all, share the same kind of pride. He got up and said:

"This is confidential material, it would be completely against the rules for me to let you have a copy." And as he was saying this, he placed the photo in the photocopier in his office. "But you might well have made a photocopy here in my absence, without my knowing, when I left the room for a moment." And he held out the sheet of paper with the blurred, imperfect reproduction, but a reproduction nonetheless. It would only last a few years, photocopies always fade, you forget how pale they become.

Now two of those years have passed, and only in the months immediately after Dorta's death did I continue thinking about that night, my sense of horror lasted rather longer than the delight and malice of the impatient press and forgetful television, there's not much you can do when there's no help, no new leads, and the media don't even serve as a reminder. It wasn't that I needed it personally, very few things fade in me: there isn't a day when I don't remember my childhood friend, there isn't a day when, at some moment, for some reason, I don't stop to think about him, you don't cease depending on people for the accidental fact that you can't see them any more. Sometimes I think that the fact is not only accidental, but insignificant, habit and the accumulated past are enough for the sense of their presence to prevail and thus never disappear, how could you not miss all of that. But it does eventually fade if you don't get to the bottom of things, worse, it can colour what went before. You know about the ending, but it's no longer in the foreground. It wasn't like that in the first months, when nightmares overwhelm sleep and the days all begin with the same insistent image, which seems like something imagined and nevertheless belongs to what actually happened, you realize it as you're cleaning your teeth, while you're shaving: "God, I'm an idiot, it really did happen." I went over and over the conversation at our last supper together, and after a period spent endowing everything with significance, the razor edge of repetition made me see that nothing was significant. Dorta liked pretending to be an eccentric, but he did not believe in magic of any kind nor in any beyond-the-grave experiences, not even in chance, no more than I do, and I hardly believe in anything. I soon concluded, if indeed I had ever doubted it, that the story of the auction in London was purely anecdotal, the sort of thing that he liked to invent or do simply in order to tell people about it afterwards, me or others, the ignorant young men he idolized or his society ladies, knowing that they would be amused. The fact that he had bid for a magic ring belonging to that crazy demonologist Crowley proved it: it was so much more colourful to recount his struggle for that particular object than for an autographed letter belonging to Wilde or Dickens or Conan Doyle. A zebra. And yet he didn't succeed in buying it, it would have been even more absurd if the joke had cost him an unexpectedly large sum of money. Perhaps the Germanic gentleman in the cowboy boots never even existed, pure imagination. And even if he had made off with the emerald: there was no question of dreaming up persecutions or sects, or Tutankhamen-type revenges or Fu Manchu-type plots, everything has its limits, even the inexplicable.

A couple of months later – by then, the press were no longer interested and it was doubtful that the police would do anything more – a possibility occurred to me that was so obvious I couldn't understand why I hadn't thought of it before. I phoned Gómez Alday and told him I wanted to see him. He sounded bored and tried to get me to tell him about my discovery over the phone, he was very pushed for time. I insisted and he arranged to see me in his office the following morning, ten minutes, he warned me, that was all the time he could spare for some hypothesis that would only further complicate his life. He also warned me that, whatever it was, he would treat it with scepticism, it all seemed perfectly clear to him, it simply wasn't that easy to find the spear-thrower: there were a lot of fingerprints on the spear, doubtless mine as well, almost everyone who visited Dorta's house had touched it or picked it up or brandished it for a moment when they saw it protruding from the umbrella stand in the hall. The inspector was sporting a healthy tan and more hair, I wasn't sure whether he had taken advantage of the August break to have an implant or if it was just a more bouffant, artistic arrangement of his normal Roman coiffure. While I talked to him, his eyes remained opaque, like a sleeping animal whose pupils can be seen through its eyelids.

"Look, I don't know much about what my friend got up to, he told me things sometimes, but never went into detail. But I can't discount the possibility that he might have paid some of these boys he went with. Apparently some of them often pretended to be heterosexual, they would accept his offer just this once, or so they said, they took pains to make it absolutely clear that normally they only went with women. That night my friend might have taken a fancy to someone like that, and the guy might have said to him that either he got him a woman as well or there was nothing doing. I can just imagine my friend shoving the boy into a taxi and patiently trawling the Castellana. I think it might even have amused him, asking the boy what he thought of that one or this one, giving his own views as if they were two bosom buddies out on the town, a couple of cock-hounds on a Saturday night. Finally, they pick up the Cuban woman and the three of them go back to his place. The boy insists that Dorta screws her so that he

can watch, or something like that. My friend's appetites are not
unlimited, given his inclinations, but he lies back and lets the
woman get on with it, just to please the boy and to get what he
wants later on. The bloke gets hysterical when it's his turn to
perform, he gets violent, he grabs the spear, which had taken his
fancy when he first came into the apartment, or perhaps they'd
already brought it into the bedroom, at Dorta's own sugges-
tion, so that the boy could pose with it like a statue, Dorta
liked playing games like that. And then the boy kills both of
them, because he's feeling trapped, even though he'd agreed to
the whole thing. It must happen all the time, mustn't it, people
suddenly getting cold feet? They lose their nerve when they see
that there's no turning back. You must know of such cases. I've
given it a lot of thought and it seems perfectly possible to me,
it would explain a lot of things which otherwise just don't fit."

Gómez Alday's eyes remained misty and lazy, but he spoke in
a tone of irritation and scorn:

"A fine friend you are. What have you got against him, all you
seem to do is to shovel more and more shit onto his corpse,
honestly, the stories you dream up, you're sick in the head you
are," he said. It wasn't that I knew a lot about these matters, but
the inspector had never heard of these perfectly run-of-the-mill
nocturnal deals and practices. The demands that were made. His
masculine pride must be of a purer sort than mine, I thought.
"But it isn't even any use to me as elaborate shit, you lack a certain
piece of information that came to light a few days ago. Your
friend did not, in fact, arrive home alone in a taxi, he was with
the whore, and the two of them were already making a spectacle
of themselves, according to the taxi driver, the woman had her
tits out and your friend was egging her on. He came and told
us this when he read about the murder and saw Dorta's photo in
the newspaper. So the spear-thrower must have arrived later on:

the pimp in pursuit of the whore or the wife, unless they were both, husband and pimp, wife and whore. Like I said before."

"He might have been in the apartment already," I said, stung by the unfairness of the reprimand. "When they failed to get it on, the guy probably forced my friend to go out hunting alone and bring him back a woman."

"Oh yes, and I suppose your friend would have gone out to trawl the streets, leaving the guy alone in the apartment?"

I thought about that. Dorta was fearful and cautious. He might go a bit crazy one night, but not to the point of allowing some rent-boy to rip him off while he went in search of a woman.

"I suppose not," I replied, exasperated. "I don't know, perhaps he phoned the rent-boy and had him come over later, the small ads section in the newspapers is full of all kinds of different services at any time of day or night."

Gómez Alday gave me another of his fulminating looks, but this time it was more out of impatience than anything else.

"So what was the woman there for, tell me that? Why would he have taken her home with him, eh? Why do you insist on trying to put all the blame on a queer. What have you got against them?"

"I've never had anything against them. My best friend was what you've just said, I mean he often got called that. If you don't believe me, ask someone else, ask other writers, they'll tell you, they love a good gossip. Ask in the gay dives, to use your term. I spent my whole life defending him."

"I find it hard to believe that you were his friend at all. Besides, I've already told you that I'm only interested in his last night, not in any other night. That's the only thing that concerns me. Now, come on, get out of here."

I went over to the door. I already had my hand on the door handle when I turned round and said:

"Who found the bodies? They found them at night didn't

they, the following night? Who went up to the apartment? Why did anyone go up?"

"We did," said Gómez Alday. "A man phoned, he said we'd find them there rotting like two dead animals, that's what he said, two animals. Probably the husband got in a state thinking about his whore lying there with a great gaping wound in her and with no one knowing anything about it. He probably came over all sentimental again. He hung up immediately after giving us the address, he wasn't much use." The inspector spun his chair round and turned his back to me as if, with that response, he was bringing any dealings with me to a close. I saw the broad nape of his neck as he said again: "Get out."

I stopped thinking about it, I assumed that the police would never clear the matter up. I stopped thinking about it for two years, until now, until one night when I'd arranged to have supper with another friend, Ruibérriz de Torres, not such an old friend as Dorta and very different, he always goes with women and they treat him well and he's not in the least bit timid, still less resigned. He's a complete scoundrel and I get on very well with him, although I know that one day he will make me the object of the same disloyalty with which he treats everyone, and that will be an end of our comradeship. He knows everything that's happening in Madrid, he goes everywhere, he knows or can arrange to get to know anyone you care to mention, he's a man of great resourcefulness, his only problem is that his criminal tendencies and his fraudulent desires are written all over his face.

We were having supper in La Ancha, on the summer terrace, sitting opposite each other, his head and body blocking my view of the table behind, a table I had no reason to be interested in until the woman sitting in the place occupied by Ruibérriz, that is, in the seat opposite mine, bent to the side to recover her napkin, snatched up by a sudden slight breeze. She leaned to

her left looking straight ahead, as we do when we pick up something that is within our reach and when we know exactly where it
has fallen. Nevertheless, she tried and failed and that was why she
had to feel for some seconds with her fingers, all the time looking
straight at us, I mean straight at where we were, because I don't
think she was actually looking at anything. It was a matter of
seconds – one, two, three and four; or five – long enough for
me to see her face and her long neck tensed in that minimal
effort of search and recovery – her tongue in one corner of her
mouth – a very long neck, perhaps made longer by the effect
of her low-cut summer dress, a small, round chin and flared
nostrils, thick eyelashes and thin eyebrows as if they had been
pencilled in, a full mouth and high cheekbones, and dark skin,
whether naturally so or from the swimming pool or the beach it
was difficult to say at first glance, although my first glance at
someone may sometimes be like a caress, at others more like a
glancing blow. Her hair was black and coiffed and curly, I saw
a necklace or a chain, I noticed the rectangular neckline, a dress
with shoulder straps, white like the dress, and heard the clink of
bracelets. I barely noticed her eyes, or perhaps I just ignored
them because I was used to not seeing them in the photograph,
in which they were screwed up, tight closed in that grimace of
pain, of someone who has died from a terrible wound. It's true
that, in summer, women look more alike than in winter and in
spring, and still more to Europeans if they are or appear to be
American, they all look the same to us, it happens a lot in summer,
on certain nights we can't tell them apart. But she really did look
like her. I know that's saying a lot, the resemblance between a
flesh-and-blood woman in motion and a mere photocopy from
the police station, between brilliant colours and murky black
and white, between laughter and paralysis, between gleaming
white teeth and some decayed molars that were never even seen,

only described, between a fully-clothed woman with no apparent money problems and an indigent, naked one, between a living woman and a dead one, between a low-cut summer dress and a wound in the chest, between a talkative tongue and the eternal silence of cracked lips, between open, smiling eyes and closed eyes. Yet she did look like her, so much so that I couldn't take my eyes off her, I immediately shifted my chair to one side, to my right, and since, even like that, I could still only half-see her and then only intermittently – concealed by Ruibérriz and by her companion, both of whom kept moving – I simply changed places altogether on the pretext that the breeze was bothering me, and I went to sit – having moved my dessert plate as well as spoon, fork and glasses – to the left of my friend, in order to enjoy an unobstructed view and I then quite openly stared. Ruibérriz realized at once that something was going on, he doesn't miss much, so I said to him, knowing that he would prove understanding about such an access of interest:

"There's a woman over there whom I find absolutely fascinating. I know it's a lot to ask, but don't turn round until I tell you. More than that, I must warn you that if she and the man she's having supper with get up, I'm going to shoot off after them, and if not, I'll wait however long it takes for them to finish and then do the same. If you want you can come with me, otherwise, you stay and we'll settle up later."

Ruibérriz de Torres smoothed his hair flirtatiously. He had only to discover that there was an interesting woman in the vicinity for him to start oozing virility and getting terribly full of himself. Even though she couldn't see him nor he her; all a bit animalesque really, his chest swelled beneath his polo shirt.

"Is she that special?" he asked restlessly, dying to turn round. From then on it would be impossible to talk about anything else, and it was my fault, I couldn't take my eyes off the woman.

"You might not think so," I said. "But I think she might be special to me, very special indeed."

Now I could see her companion in three-quarters profile, a man of about fifty who looked rich and rather coarse, if she was a prostitute, he was obviously inexperienced and didn't know that you could get straight down to business, without the need for supper on a restaurant terrace. If she wasn't, then it was justifiable, what would be less so was that the woman had agreed to go out with such an unattractive man, although I've always found the choices women make as regards their flirtations and their love affairs a complete mystery, sometimes, by my lights, a complete aberration. One thing was certain, they weren't married or engaged or anything, I mean it was clear that they had not yet lain together, to use the old expression. The man was trying too hard to be pleasant and attentive: he was careful to keep filling her glass, he prattled on, recounting anecdotes or giving his opinions about things so as not to fall into the silence that discourages any contact, he lit cigarettes for her with a windproof lighter, like the ones you get in cars, Spanish men don't go to all that trouble unless they want something, they don't watch their manners.

As I continued to look at her, my initial confidence began to wane, as always happens: certainty is followed by doubt and uncertainty by ratification, usually only when it's too late. I suppose that, as the minutes passed, the image of the living woman became superimposed on that of the dead woman, displacing or blurring it, thus allowing for less comparison, less similarity. She behaved like a woman of easy virtue, which didn't mean that she was, as far as I was concerned, she couldn't be, since, as far as I was concerned, she still lay beneath the desolation of the lights and the television left on all day and of the semen in her mouth – entirely unmerited – and the hole in her chest, which she had merited even less. I looked at her, I looked at her breasts, I looked at them out of habit and also because they were the part of the murdered woman I was most familiar with, aside from her face, I tried to get some sense of recognition, but it was impossible, they were covered by her bra and her dress, although I could glimpse her cleavage beneath her neckline which was neither sober nor exaggerated. I was suddenly gripped by the indecent thought that I had to see what those breasts were like, I was sure I would recognize them if I saw them uncovered. It would be no easy task, especially not that night, when her companion would have exactly the same intentions and would not want to surrender his place to me.

Suddenly I smelled something, a sweet, cloying smell, an unmistakable aroma, I don't know if it was a change in the direction of the wind that wafted it to me for the first time – the wind swinging round – or if it was the first clove-scented cigarette that had been smoked at the table next to ours, a different, better-quality cigarette to be smoked with the coffee or the liqueur, like someone treating themselves to a cigar. I glanced at the man's hands, I saw his right hand, it was playing with the lighter. The woman had a cigarette in her left hand, and the man then raised his left arm in order to gesture to the waiter, asking for the bill, his hand was empty, therefore, at that moment, the exotic smell was coming from her, she was smoking an Indonesian Gudang Garam that crackles as it slowly burns down, I had had a packet myself two years before, Dorta's final gift to me, and I had made it last, but not that long, a month after he'd given it to me it was finished, I smoked the last cigarette in his memory, well, each and every one of them really, I kept the empty red packet, "Smoking kills", that's what it says. How was it possible that she – if it was her – had made the cigarettes that my friend must also have given her that same night last so long.

Two years, those "kretek" cigarettes would be dry as sawdust now, an open packet, yet they still gave off a pungent perfume.

"Can you smell what I smell?" I asked Ruibérriz, who was beginning to get fed up.

"Can I look at her now?" he said.

"Can you smell it?" I insisted.

"Yes, is someone smoking incense or something?"

"It's cloves," I said. "Tobacco with cloves."

The man's gesture to the waiter allowed me to make the same gesture of writing in the air to another waiter and so be ready when the couple got up. Only then did I give permission to Ruibérriz to turn round; he did so and decided to accompany me. We followed a few paces behind the couple, I saw the woman standing up for the first time – a short skirt, open-toed shoes, painted toenails – and as we took those steps, I also heard her name, the name that she had never had for me or for Gómez Alday nor perhaps for Dorta. "You're a lovely mover, Estela," said the coarse man, not so coarse that he wasn't absolutely right in his remark, which was spoken more in admiration than by way of being an amorous compliment. Ruibérriz and I separated for a moment, he went over to the car in order to pick me up as soon as they got in theirs, they weren't travelling by taxi. When they did so, I got into our car and we drove off after them, keeping a short distance behind, there wasn't much traffic, but enough for them not to notice us. It was a brief journey, they drove to an area of suburban houses, the street was called Torpedero Tucumán, a comical address to send a letter to. They parked and went into one of the houses, a three-storey house, lights were lit on every storey, as if there were already plenty of people there, perhaps they were going to a party, supper followed by a party, that guy was really going to a lot of trouble.

Ruibérriz and I parked the car and stayed where we were for

the moment, from there we could see the lights but nothing else, most of the blinds were pulled halfway down and there were lace curtains that didn't move in the wind, you'd have to go right up to one of the windows on the ground floor and peer through a crack, we might even end up doing that, I thought quickly. It immediately seemed to us, though, that it couldn't be a party, because there was no music drifting out through open windows, no sounds of anarchic conversations or laughter. The blinds were only up on two windows on the third floor and you couldn't see anyone in there, just a standard lamp, and walls without books or pictures.

"What do you think?" I asked Ruibérriz.

"I don't think they'll stay very long. There's not much fun to be had in that house, apart from the intimate kind, and those two aren't going to spend the night together, not there at least, whatever kind of place it is. Did you see who opened the door, did they have a key or did they knock?"

"I couldn't see, but I don't think they knocked."

"It might be his house, and if it is, then she'll be out again in a couple of hours, no longer than that. It might be her place, in which case, he'll be the one to come out, much sooner too, say about an hour. It might be a massage parlour, that's what they like to call them now, and then again he'll be the one to leave, but give him about thirty or forty-five minutes. Lastly, there might be a few select poker games going on, but I don't think so. Only then would they spend the night there, losing and recovering what they'd lost. No, I don't think it's likely to be her house. No, it can't be."

Ruibérriz knows all the different territories in the city, he has experience and a good eye. He doesn't need to ask many questions and he can find out anything or locate anyone with a couple of phone calls and perhaps a couple more made by his contacts.

"Why don't you find out for me whose house it is? I'll wait here, in case one or other leaves unexpectedly. It wouldn't take you long to find out, I'm sure."

He sat there looking at me, his tanned arms resting on the steering wheel.

"What is it with this woman? What are you after? I didn't get a very good look at her, but I don't know that she's worth all this fuss."

"Not for you probably, as I said. Just let me see what happens tonight and I'll tell you the whole story another day. I just need to know where she lives, where she hangs out or where she's going to be sleeping tonight, when she does finally go to bed."

"This isn't the first time you've asked me to wait for a story, I don't know if you realize that."

"But it'll probably be the last," I said. If I told him straight out that I thought I might be seeing a dead woman, it was quite likely that he wouldn't help me at all, things like that make him nervous, as they do me normally, we who hardly believe in anything.

I got out of the car and Ruibérriz drove off to make his enquiries. There were no shops or cinemas or bars in that area, a boring, tree-lined residential street, with barely any lighting, with nothing you could use as a pretext or to distract yourself while you were waiting. If a neighbour saw me, he would doubtless take me for a marauder, there was no reason why I should be there, alone, silent, smoking. I crossed to the other side of the street just in case I could see anything of the upper storey from there, the only one where the windows were unobstructed. I did see something, but only briefly, a large woman, who was not Estela, passing and disappearing and passing again in the opposite direction after a few seconds and then disappearing again, obscuring my view still more after she had gone, since, when she

left the room, she switched off the light: as if she had just gone
in there for a moment to pick something up. I crossed the road
again and approached the gate as stealthily as an old-fashioned
thief; I pushed and it gave way, it was open, people leave it like
that when there's a party on or if a lot of people come and go.
I continued to advance so carefully that had I been treading
on sand there would have been no footprints, I moved slowly
towards one of the windows on the ground floor, the one to the
left of the front door from where I was standing. As with nearly
all the windows, the blind was down but the slats were open to let
in the warm breeze that had slackened now, that is, they weren't
tight shut. Behind the blinds there were motionless lace curtains,
the room must be air-conditioned or perhaps it was a sauna. You
often unwittingly take steps that you consider possible merely
because they are possible and it has occurred to you to take
them, and that is how so many acts and so many murders are
committed, sometimes the idea leads to the act as if it could not
live and sustain itself as long as it was a mere idea, as if there
were a certain kind of possibility that grows frustrated and begins
to fade if it is not instantly put into action, without our realizing
that, in that way too, it has vanished and died, it will no longer
be a possibility, but a past event. I found myself in the situation
I had foreseen in the car, with my eyes glued to a crack at
about eye level, looking, peering, trying to make out something
through the tiny gap and through the transparent white cloth
that made it even harder to see. That room too was only dimly
lit, a large part of it lay in shadow, it was like trying to get to
the bottom of a story from which the main elements have been
deliberately omitted and about which we know only odd details,
my vision blurred and with only a restricted view.

But I thought I saw them and I did, both of them, Estela
and the coarse man one on top of the other, outside the beam

of the light, the niceties were over, on a bed or perhaps it was a mattress or the floor, at first I couldn't even make out who was who, two dark, intertwined masses of flesh, someone was naked in there, I said to myself, the woman would have uncovered those breasts that I so needed to see, or perhaps not, perhaps not, she might still have her bra on. There was movement or was it struggle, but hardly any sound emerged, no grunts or cries or groans of pleasure or laughter, like a scene from a silent movie that would never have been shown in decent cinemas, a grim, muffled effort of bodies doubtless entering upon what was just another stage in the proceedings – the fuck – rather than a surrender to genuine desire, his body felt no more desire than hers did, but it was difficult to say where the one began and the other ended or which was which, given the darkness and the veil of the curtain, they were just a grotesque shape, how could I possibly not be able to distinguish the body of a young woman from that of a coarse man? Suddenly a torso and a head with a hat on loomed into view, they entered the beam of light for a moment before plunging down again, the man had donned a cowboy hat in order to have a fuck, good grief, I thought, what a jerk. So he was the one who was on top or above, when he rose up, I thought I also saw his hairy, swarthy, unpleasant torso, broad and undelineated, not exactly athletic. I looked through the slat below to see if I could catch a glimpse of the woman and her breasts, but I couldn't see anything and so returned to the slat above, hoping that the man might grow tired and want to rest underneath, it was odd not knowing if it was a bed or a mattress or the floor, and even odder how muffled the sound was, a silence like a gag. Then I noticed a new singlemindedness about the sweating, two-headed beast into which they had been momentarily transformed, they're going to change position, I thought, they're going to change places in order to prolong this stage of the proceedings, which is just that, another stage, since the participants remain the same.

I heard the bolt on the door and scuttled off to the left, just managing to disappear round the corner of the house before I heard a woman's voice saying goodbye to some people who were leaving ("Bye then, come back and see us again sometime," as if she were an American): a literary critic I know by sight, with a pure primate face and wearing red trousers and hiking boots, another jerk, if that *was* a whorehouse it didn't surprise me in the least that he should visit it, he always has to pay, like his friend, a fat guy with a greying crewcut, a head like an inverted egg and a reptilian mouth, wearing glasses and a tie. They swaggered out and ostentatiously slammed the gate shut, no one would see them, the street was empty and dark, the second guy sounded as if he came from the Canaries, another jerk to judge by his appearance and his behaviour, a bit of a flash harry. When I could no longer hear their footsteps, I returned to my post, a couple of minutes or three or four had passed and now the man and Estela were no longer intertwined, they had not changed position, but they had stopped, the end or a pause. The man was standing up, or kneeling on the mattress, the beam of light illuminated him more than it did her, reclining or sitting, I could see the back of her head, the coarse man grabbed her head with his two hands and made her turn it a little, now I could see both their faces and his erect body with its proliferating hair and his ridiculous hat, it seemed to me he was starting to squeeze Estela's face with his two thumbs, how strong two thumbs can be, it was as if he were caressing her, but hurting her too, as if he were digging into her high cheekbones or giving her a cruel massage that went ever deeper, becoming more and more intense, he was pushing into her cheekbones as if he wanted to crush them. I felt alarmed, I thought for a moment that he was going to kill her

and he couldn't kill her because she was already dead and because
I had to see her breasts and talk to her about something, ask her
about the spear or the wound – the weapon wasn't left impaled
in her, someone had pulled it out – and about my friend Dorta
who had received her blood on that spear. The man eased the
pressure, let her go, he squeezed his knuckles and cracked them,
muttered a few words, then moved away, perhaps it was nothing,
perhaps it was just the reminder some men like to give women
that they could hurt them if they wanted to. He took off his
hat, threw it on the floor as if he no longer needed it, and picked
up his clothes from a chair, he would be the one to leave. She lay
back, absolutely still, she didn't appear to be hurt, or perhaps
she was used to being treated violently.

"Víctor!" I heard Ruibérriz's voice calling to me quietly from
the other side of the gate. I hadn't heard him arrive, or his car.

With my head turned towards the house – sometimes it's hard
to make yourself look away – I went to meet him as daintily as
I had come, I took him by the sleeve and dragged him over to
the other pavement.

"So," I said, "what did you find out?"

"The usual, it's a whorehouse, open all hours, they advertise
in the newspapers, superchicks, European, Latin American and
Asian, they say, amongst other things. I warn you there'll be
hardly a soul in there. In the phone book it's listed under the
name of Calzada Fernández, Mónica. So the man will be the one
to leave, if he hasn't already."

"He must be about ready to, they've finished and he's getting
dressed. A couple of punters with pretensions to being literary types have just left, they probably fancy themselves as real
Renaissance men," I said. "We'll have to skedaddle in a minute,
but I'm going in there as soon as he comes out."

"What, have you gone mad? You're going to follow in the

footsteps of that hick? What is it with you and that woman?"

I again tugged him by the sleeve and dragged him further off, beneath the trees, where we would be invisible to anyone coming out. A lazy neighbourhood dog barked and immediately fell silent. Only then did I answer Ruibérriz.

"It's not at all what you're thinking, but I have to get a look at her breasts tonight, that's all that matters. And if she is a whore then all the better, I'll pay her, I'll have a good look at them, we might talk for a bit, and then I'll leave."

"You might talk for a bit and then leave? You can't be serious. She's nothing very special it's true, but she's worth more than just a look. What's with her breasts?"

"Nothing, I'll tell you tomorrow because there may well be nothing to tell anyway. If you want to follow the guy in the car when he leaves, fine, although I don't think you need bother. If not, thanks for the research and now please go, I'll be all right on my own. Is there nothing you can't find out?"

Ruibérriz looked at me impatiently despite that final bit of flattery. But he usually puts up with me, he's a friend. Until the day he ceases to be.

"I don't give a damn about the guy, or her for that matter. If you're OK, then stay, you can tell me about it tomorrow. But be careful, you're not used to these places."

Ruibérriz left and this time I did hear his car in the distance while the door of the house opened (maybe the woman again said "Come back and see us again sometime", I couldn't hear from where I was). I saw that the coarse man was outside the house now, I heard the noisy gate. He walked wearily in the opposite direction – his night of pretence and effort over – I could approach now behind him while he disappeared off amongst the black foliage in search of his car. I felt intensely impatient, and yet I waited a few moments longer, smoking another cigarette before pushing open the gate. There was still a light on in the bedroom where the encounter had taken place, the same lamp, the blind still lowered, but with the slats open, they didn't air the rooms immediately.

I rang the bell, it was an old-fashioned bell, not chimes. I waited. I waited and a large woman opened the door to me, I'd seen her on the third floor, she was like one of our aunts when we were little, Dorta's aunts or my aunts, fresh from the 1960s even down to her platinum blonde, flying-saucer hairstyle or her make-up, courtesy of eyebrow pencil, powder and even tweezers.

"Good evening," she said interrogatively.

"I'd like to see Estela."

"She's having a shower," she said quite naturally, and added guilelessly, displaying an excellent memory: "You haven't been here before."

"No, a friend of mine told me about her. I'm just passing through Madrid and a friend of mine spoke well of her."

"Ah," she said, drawing out the vowel, she had a Galician accent, "I'll see what we can do. You'll have to wait a moment, though. Come in."

A small room in near darkness with two sofas facing each other, you walked straight in there from the hallway, all you had to do was to keep walking. The walls were almost empty, not a book or a painting, just a blown-up photo stuck on a thick piece of board, like they used to have in airports and travel agencies. It was a photograph of white skyscrapers, the title left no room for doubt, Caracas, I've never been to Caracas. I immediately thought, perhaps Estela is Venezuelan, but Venezuelan women don't have soft breasts, at least they don't have that reputation. Perhaps Estela didn't either, perhaps she wasn't the dead woman and it was all just a mirage born of alcohol and the summer and the night, a lot of beer with a dash of lemon juice and too much heat, if only it was, I thought, stories already absorbed by time should not subsequently change, if in their day, they've been filed away without explanation: the lack of any explanation ends up becoming the story itself, if the story has already been absorbed by time. I sat down, Aunt Mónica left me alone, "I'll go and see how long she'll be," she said. I awaited her return, I knew that she would return before the person I wanted to see, the lady was her aide-de-camp. And yet that isn't what happened, the lady didn't come back for ages, she didn't come back at all, I felt like looking for the bathroom where the prostitute was having a shower and simply going in and seeing her without waiting any longer, but I'd only frighten her, and after I'd smoked two cigarettes, she was the one who came down the stairs with her hair uncombed and wet, wearing a bathrobe but still in her street shoes, open-toed, her nails painted, the buckles loose as the only sign that her feet were also at home, off duty. Her bathrobe was not yellow, but sky blue.

"Are you in much of a hurry?" she asked point-blank.

"Yes." I didn't mind what she understood by that, after a while, she would understand everything, and she would be the one obliged to give me an explanation. She looked at me with absolutely no curiosity, without really looking, not like Gómez Alday did, but like someone who, given her situation, expects no surprises. She was an imperfectly pretty woman, or, rather, she was pretty despite her imperfections, at least in the summer.

"Do you want me to get dressed or am I all right like this?" she said, immediately calling me 'tú', perhaps she felt she had the right to when she knew I was in a hurry. To get dressed in order to get undressed, I thought, just in case I wanted to see the second part.

"You're fine as you are."

She said nothing more, she gestured with her head towards one of the doors on the ground floor and walked towards it like a clerk going to look for a file, she opened the door. I stood up and followed her at once, she must have noticed my evident impatience, it didn't seem to frighten her, rather it made her feel superior to me, she was condescending in her manner, a big mistake if it really *was* her and she had to answer for a night that was now old and perhaps forgotten. We went in, it was the same room, still unaired, in which she had just been grappling with the coarse man, there was an acidic smell, but it was much more bearable than one might have supposed. A fan turned on the ceiling, through my slat I hadn't been able to see it. There was the cowboy hat, thrown on the floor, perhaps for use by clients with complexes or with a head like an inverted egg, the hat was for hire too. There had been a cowboy element in Dorta's last night too, he had spoken to me of some peculiar crocodile-skin cowboy boots.

She sat on the bed that was neither a mattress nor a bed, one of those low Japanese affairs that I can't remember the name of, I believe they're fashionable.

"Did she tell you how much it is?" she asked. The question was lacklustre, mechanical.

"No, but it doesn't matter, we can discuss that later. There'll be no problem."

"With the lady," said Estela. "You discuss it with the lady." And she added: "Right, what do you want? Apart from it being quick."

"Undo your bathrobe."

She obeyed, she untied the belt allowing me to see something, but not enough. She seemed bored, even irritated, if before there had been no desire, now there was tacit rejection. Her accent was Central American or Caribbean, doubtless hardened by several years in Madrid.

"Open it more, right open, so that I can see you," I said, and my voice must have sounded odd, because she looked at me properly for the first time, slightly apprehensively. But she undid

the bathrobe, so wide that she revealed even her shoulders, like
an old-fashioned movie star at a gala performance, not much of
a gala performance tonight, there they were, those breasts so
familiar in black and white, I recognized them in colour too
without a moment's hesitation, despite the darkness, the provocative, shapely, but, nevertheless, soft breasts, they would give in
the hand like bags of water, she was too poor to consider plastic
surgery, for two years I had looked at them, all bloodstained, in
a slowly fading photocopy, more often than I should have, more
often than I had imagined I would when I made my extravagant,
macabre request to Gómez Alday, he was an understanding man.
On her breasts, where the skin was not quite as dark as elsewhere,
there was no wound or cut or scar or gash, her skin was uniform
and smooth, unmarked apart from her nipples, too dark for my
taste, one gets used to knowing at a glance what one likes and
what one doesn't.

I was immediately assailed by far too many thoughts, the
woman alive and therefore still alive, the look of pain in the photo,
the screwed-up eyes and the gritted teeth, those closed eyes
were not the eyes of a dead woman because the dead no longer
struggle and everything ceases when they expire, even pain, why
had it not occurred to me that her expression was of someone
alive or of someone dying, but never of someone dead. And why
the knickers, why was her corpse wearing knickers, why preserve
one item of clothing when you've gone that far, only someone
still alive keeps her knickers on. And if she was alive, my best
friend might be alive too, Dorta the joker, Dorta the resigned,
what kind of joke had he played on me making me believe in his
murder and in his condemnation, what kind of joke was that if
he were still alive?

"Where did you get those cigarettes from?" I asked.

"What cigarettes?" Estela was immediately on the alert, and to gain time she said once more: "What cigarettes?"

"The ones you were smoking before, in the restaurant, the ones that smell of cloves. Let me see the packet."

She instinctively closed her bathrobe, without tying the belt, as if to protect herself from discovery, this was a man who had watched her and followed her from La Ancha or perhaps before that, perhaps all night. My voice must have sounded rather nervous and angry, because she pointed to a handbag left on a chair, the chair that had borne the clothes of the coarse man.

"They're in there. A friend gave them to me."

I'd made her feel afraid, I saw that she was afraid of me and that she would therefore do whatever I asked her to. There was no more superiority or condescension, just fear of me and of my hands, or of a sharp weapon that might pierce or tear her. I picked up the bag, opened it and took out the slim red and gold and black packet, with its design of curved rails in relief and its message, "Smoking kills". Kretek.

"What friend? The one who was with you? Who is he?"

"I don't know who he is, he wanted to go out to supper tonight, I've only been with him once before."

How I hate men who hurt women and now I hated myself – or I did afterwards – when I grabbed Estela's arm and snatched open her bathrobe again, leaving her unprotected, and I ran my thumb between her breasts as if I wanted to draw something out of there, I did so several times, pressing hard and saying:

"Where's the wound, eh? Where's the spear, eh? Where's all the blood, what happened to my friend, who killed him, you killed him. Who put his glasses on him, tell me, you did, whose idea was it, yours?"

I held her immobilized with her arm twisted, twisted up her back, and with my other hand, with my strong thumb, I was pressing against her sternum, up and down, crushing it, or rubbing

it, feeling on either side the actual touch of those breasts I had
seen so often with my tactile eyes.

"I don't know anything about what happened, they didn't
tell me," she said, whimpering, "he was already dead when I
got there. They just called me in to do the photos."

"They? Who did? When?"

You never know what your thumbs might do, someone who
might have been watching me through the slats in the blinds
would have felt alarmed, other people's thumbs seem unstoppable
or uncontrollable and as if it will always be too late. But these
were my thumbs. I realized that there was no need to frighten
her any more or hurt her any more, I stopped, I let her go, I
noticed that my thumbs were hot from the rubbing, as if momentarily on fire, she would feel that same burning sensation between
her breasts like a warning and a reminder, she would tell me
everything she knew. But before she spoke, before she recovered
and spoke, the idea had already crossed my mind, why had they
found him the following night, so late and after such a long delay,
the two corpses that were only one, perhaps in order to plan and
prepare it all and take the photos, and who took those photos that
were never published, not even the one of her, not even her face
half-covered by her hair, pulled forward by her own living hand,
just pictures of my friend Dorta in better times, it was a set-up
that hair slightly covering her face, the news just said what the
police had said, there was no evidence from neighbours and I
alone saw the photos, and only in Gómez Alday's office, only a
judge would have seen them otherwise.

"The police called me. The inspector called me, he said he
needed me to pose with the body of a man who had died a violent
death. You have to do all kinds of things sometimes, even lie
down next to a dead man. The dead man was already dead, I
promise you, I didn't do anything with him."

Dorta was dead. For a few moments he had returned to life
in my suspicious mind, not so very strange really: habit and the
accumulated past are enough for the feeling of presence never to
fade, not seeing someone can be accidental, even insignificant,
and there isn't a day when I don't remember my childhood
friend with whom no woman ever did anything, either alive or
dead, that worried Estela, the poor thing: "The dead man was
already dead, I promise you"; and there was no mingling of
blood, no semen, no anything, it had all been invented by Gómez
Alday to tell me or any other interested party or busybody so
that I would absorb it in time, newspapers soon tire and they
didn't give that many details, they said only that sex had taken
place between the two corpses before they had become corpses.

"They made a fine mess of you, didn't they? Those great gobs
of blood and everything."

"Yes, they put tomato ketchup on my chest and waited for it
to dry and then they took the photos later. It didn't take long,
it was hot, it soon dried, the young man did it. They gave me a
few thousand pesetas and told me to keep my mouth shut."
She made a gesture with her thumb closing her mouth, as if with
a zip. She went on talking, but she was less frightened now,
she wouldn't stop talking because of that, although she would
have noticed that the expression or thought "poor thing" had
passed through my mind, we all notice that, and that makes us
feel easier. "It happened ages ago. If you talk, I'll have you
flogged and send you back to Cuba in a slave ship, he said, the
inspector that is. And now what will happen, now what, they'll
send me back to Cuba."

"The young man," I said, and my voice sounded even odder,
she might not yet be entirely safe from me, "What young man.
What young man?"

"The boy who was there with him all the time, he was doing

his military service, he had to get back to the barracks, they talked about that." And Gómez Alday, I thought, had had the nerve to say that the spear-thrower might be someone used to sticking bayonets in people, may your heart rot full of iron, even though we're not at war, just another sack, a sack of flour sack of feathers sack of meat, kretek kretek. "That's all I know, I arrived and left again in the evening, with my money and the cigarettes, I stole those from the house on my way out, when they weren't looking, two cartons. I've still got three or four packets left, I smoke them slowly, it impresses people, they still smell really strong."

Her motive for smoking them was not very different from Dorta's, they had something in common, he and Estela. I sat down beside her on the low bed and I stroked her shoulder.

"I'm sorry," I said. "The dead man was my friend and I saw those photos."

Ruibérriz de Torres is right far too often, he knows us all too well. After all, every now and then, over a long period of time, I had seen that pained face and those still, dead, bloodstained breasts, and I was glad to see them moving and alive and newly showered, although my friend, on the other hand, was still dead and there had been so much deceit. It was also a way of paying her and recompensing the woman for the bad time I'd given her, although I could also have just given her the money anyway, in payment for the information. But then again, I wouldn't be able to sleep until it was time for offices and police stations to open, although some police stations stay open all night.

I left money in the waiting room on my way out, perhaps too much, perhaps too little, Aunt Mónica would have gone to bed hours ago. When I left, the woman was sleeping. I don't think they'll be sending her back to Cuba, as she feared.

Gómez Alday looked even better than the last time I'd seen

him, nearly two years before. He had improved with time, they'd promoted him, he must have been feeling more at ease. Now that I knew that he did not share my foolish masculine pride, I realized that he looked after himself, those of us who do have that pride take rather less care of ourselves; I had neither the time nor was I in the mood for friendly questions. He didn't refuse to see me, he didn't get up from his revolving chair when I went into his office, he merely looked at me with his veiled eyes that showed no great surprise, only, perhaps, annoyance. He remembered me.

"So what's new?" he said.

"What's new is that I've spoken to Estela, your dead woman, and not through her photograph either. I'd like to know what you have to say to me now about your spear-thrower."

The inspector passed one hand over his Roman head on which the hair seemed to be growing ever thicker, he obviously earned enough money to pay for his implants, I thought for a second, inopportune thoughts surface all the time. He picked up a pencil from his desk and drummed with it on the wood. He wasn't smoking now.

"So she decided to talk, did she?" he replied. "When she arrived she was called Miriam, if, that is, you're talking about the same Cuban whore."

"What happened? You're going to have to tell me. You didn't want to go and question those poofters, why waste time? I don't know how you had the nerve to call them that."

Gómez Alday gave a faint smile, there was perhaps even the ghost of a blush. He seemed about as alarmed as a boy who's been caught out lying. A white lie, something that will have no consequences beyond that telling off. Perhaps he knew that I wouldn't go to anyone else with the story, perhaps he knew that even before I did. He took some time to reply, but not because he

wasn't sure what to say: it was as if he were considering whether
or not I deserved to hear his confession.

"Well, you have to put up a front, don't you?" he said at last,
and paused, he was still not sure. Then he went on: "I don't know
if you're familiar with those boys, your friend probably told you
something about them. If they're very young, they have no sense
at all of loyalty or propriety, they're anyone's for a night, they
can be seduced with a few flattering remarks, never mind if it's
someone famous or they're promised a tour of a few expensive
places. They hang around, they have nothing else to do, they
hang around waiting to be seduced. They're much vainer than
women, you know." Gómez Alday stopped, he was talking as
if none of what he was saying had the least importance, as if it
belonged to the remote past, and it's true that the past becomes
more remote more quickly all the time. "Well, going back to the
one I was with at the time.Your friend picked him up one night,
in the street, I was on duty. I don't want to speak ill of him, he
was your friend, but he went too far with the boy, that wretched
spear, and the boy got frightened, your friend's little games got
him rattled, you said as much, I remember, it happens sometimes,
there are things people wish they'd never started, they can wish
that for all kinds of reasons, and they get frightened by anything
unexpected. He lost his nerve and bashed your friend on the
head, and then he speared him, as if he was sticking a bayonet
in him. He wasn't a bad boy, really he wasn't, he was doing his
military service, I haven't heard from him for some time, they
come and go, they're not in the least bit sentimental, not like
pimps or husbands. He phoned me, he was terrified, we had to set
something up to avoid suspicion falling on him." Gómez Alday
seemed momentarily vulnerable and weak, the past becomes
suddenly remote when the person who constitutes our present
disappears from our life, the thread of continuity is broken and

suddenly yesterday seems a long way away. "What can I say, what could I do but help him out, what would be gained by ruining two lives instead of just one, especially if one of those lives was over and done."

I sat looking at his rather corpulent body, he seemed tall even when sitting down. He had no difficulty holding my gaze, his somnolent eyes would never have blinked or looked away, those misty eyes would have stared me down into hell itself. There was no longer any sign of weakness in that face, it was gone in a moment.

"Who put his glasses on him?" I said at last. "Whose idea was it to put them on?"

The inspector made an impatient gesture, as if my question made him think that I hadn't, after all, deserved either the explanation or the story.

"Who cares?" he said. "Don't talk to me about pranks in the middle of a homicide case. Just ask the questions that matter."

I did as he said. "Didn't anyone want to see the body of that unusually lively dead woman? The judge, the pathologist."

He shrugged.

"Don't be so naive. Here and in the morgue we do as we like. We investigate what we want to and nobody asks any awkward questions. We had a long apprenticeship, forty years doing exactly as we pleased without ever having to answer to anyone, we can't just throw that away. I mean under Franco, perhaps you don't remember. Although it's much the same anywhere, there's no shortage of learning opportunities."

Gómez Alday wasn't entirely lacking in humour. He wasn't the kind of person you should ask such a question, but I did:

"Why did you go to such lengths for that boy? You were taking a hell of a risk even so."

There was a brief flash in those sleepy eyes, then he did what he had done once before: he spun round in his seat and turned his back on me, as if bringing to a close his sporadic dealings with me. I stared at the broad nape of his neck as he said:

"I risked everything." He fell silent for a moment and then added casually: "Haven't you ever been in love?"

I turned and opened the door to leave. I didn't reply, but I seemed to recall that I had.

IN UNCERTAIN TIME

I SAW HIM twice in the flesh and the first time was both the happiest and the most unfortunate, although it was only unfortunate retrospectively, that is, it is now but it wasn't then, so really I shouldn't say that it was. It was in the Joy discotheque, very late at night, especially for him, you imagine that a footballer should go to bed really early, always thinking about the next game, or just training and sleeping, watching videos of other teams or their own, watching themselves, their successes and failures and the missed opportunities that go on being missed for all eternity in those films, sleeping and training and eating, living the life of married babies, it's good if they have a wife who can be a mother to them and supervise their timetable. Most take no notice, they hate sleeping and hate training, and the really great players only think about the game when they actually run out onto the pitch and realize that they had better win because there are a hundred thousand people who *have* spent the whole week thinking about the confrontation or wanting vengeance against their hated rivals. For great players those rivals only exist for ninety minutes and for one reason only: they are there to stop them getting what they want, that's all. Later they would happily go out for a drink with those same adversaries, if it wasn't frowned upon. Resentment is for the mediocre players.

He, of course, was not a mediocre player and for some time it was thought that he would become a great player, once he was more mature and more focused, which never happened, or happened perhaps too late. He was Hungarian, like Kubala and Puskas and Kocsis and Czibor, but we found his surname much less easy to pronounce, it was written Szentkuthy and people ended up calling him "Kentucky", which sounded more familiar and more Spanish, which is why people sometimes rather rudely referred to him as "Fried Chicken" (which didn't tally at all with his athletic build), the bolder and more outspoken of the radio commentators allowed themselves to get carried away when he stepped on to the pitch: "For Barcelona tonight it looks like it could be out of the frying pan and into the fire." Or else: "Kentucky is really cooking with gas tonight; he's looking to give the other side a real roasting. This boy is pure boiling oil, he's hot, he's slippery and someone might just get their fingers burned!" Journalists got a lot of mileage out of him, but they have short memories.

When I bumped into him at the Joy discotheque, he had been in Madrid for a season and a half and already spoke good Spanish, very correct, though somewhat limited, with a pronounced but perfectly tolerable accent, it seems that people from Central Europe all have a facility for languages, we Spaniards are the least gifted when it comes to learning other languages or pronouncing them, that's what the Roman historians said, a people incapable of pronouncing an initial S, as in Scipio or Schillaci or Szentkuthy: Spaniards say Escipión, Esquilache, Kentucky, linguistic tendencies have changed. Szentkuthy (I'll call him by his real name, since I only have to write it not say it) had already had time to get over the novelty of a country that was new, fun and luxurious compared to his previous harsh existence, but not yet long enough to take it as natural and inevitable. Perhaps he had reached the point that follows every important attainment, when what you have achieved no longer seems to you like a mere gift or a miracle (you recognize it as an achievement) and you begin to fear for its permanence or, rather, to look with horror on any possible return to a past to which you were once resigned and which you tend therefore to erase, I am not who I was, I am only now, I come from nowhere and I do not know myself.

We were brought together at the same table by mutual acquaintances, although he only came over from time to time in order to recover his glass for a second and take a sip between dances, a form of training, a tireless athlete, at least he would have the energy to keep going for ninety minutes and into extra time. He was not a good dancer, he danced too enthusiastically and with no sense of rhythm, he lacked the necessary talent to bring harmony to his movements, and some of the people at the table were laughing at him, in this country there's an element of cruelty in every situation, even when there's no reason for it, people take pleasure in hurting or thinking that they do. He dressed better than when he had first arrived, according to the photos I saw in the press, but not as well as his Spanish colleagues, who were keener students of fashion, that is, of fashion advertisements. He was one of those men who always gives the impression that he's got his shirt hanging out of his trousers, even if he hasn't, of course, on the pitch he wore his shirt outside when the referee allowed it. He did, at last, come and sit down and, laughing and gesturing, ordered everyone else onto the dance floor so that he could watch them while he was resting, now it was his turn to have some fun, though doubtless without malice or cruelty, perhaps merely hoping to learn other movements less awkward than his own. I was the only one who did not obey him, I never dance, I just watch. He didn't insist, not because he didn't know who I was, we'd not been introduced – that didn't seem to bother him, certain that everyone knew who *he* was – but because of the definite way I said no. I shook my head the way we city-dwellers do when we refuse alms to a beggar and pass by without even slackening our pace. The comparison isn't mine, it was his:

"You look like someone refusing me alms," he said when we were alone, the others were all out on the dance floor just to please him. He used the "usted" form like any good foreigner who still sticks to the rules, his vocabulary wasn't bad, the word "alms" isn't that common.

"How do you know? Have you ever been refused alms by anyone?" I said, and I, on the other hand, called him "tú" because of the difference in age and because of an unconscious superiority complex, which I became instantly aware of and which was why I added: "Why don't we call each other 'tú'." And even that I did as if I were giving him permission.

"Who hasn't? Alms come in many different forms. I'm Szentkuthy," he said, offering me his hand. "Nobody ever introduces anybody here."

He was an intelligent chap: he behaved in accordance with reality (everyone knew who he was), but his words gave the lie to his behaviour. That is, he distinguished between the two things, which is not easy to do without appearing either unbearably hypocritical or detestably ingenuous. I told him my name, added my profession and shook his hand. He didn't ask me about that profession, so far removed from his own, he wasn't interested not even in order to make polite conversation, an unexpected and probably undesired conversation, he had hoped to be left alone at the table to watch the dancing. His fair hair was parted in the middle and combed back in two wavy, almost symmetrical blocks, as if he were the conductor of an orchestra, he had a very wide smile like a character in a comic, a rather broad nose and very small, twinkling blue eyes, like little fairy lights.

"Which one are you with?" I asked, indicating the women on the dance floor with a movement of my nay-saying head, the women had all gone up to the dance floor as a group. "Which one's your girlfriend? Which one of them are you with?" I insisted in order to make the question clearer.

He seemed to like the fact that I didn't immediately start talking about the team or the training or the championship and perhaps that's why he replied without embarrassment and with an almost childlike smile. His pride was neither offensive nor humiliating, not even to the women, he said it as if they had chosen him, not the other way round, and perhaps that's how it was:

"Of the six at the table," he said, "I've already been with three. How's that?" And he held up three fingers on his left hand, what with all the noise it wasn't easy to hear. He was still addressing me as "usted", and that reiteration made me feel rather old.

"And whose turn is it today?" I replied. "Are you going for a repeat, or having a change?"

He laughed.

"I'll only go for a repeat if there's no alternative."

"A collector, eh? What else do you collect? I mean, goals apart."

He sat thinking for a moment.

"That's all really, goals and women. A different woman for every goal, that's my way of celebrating," he said, smiling, so that it seemed a mere joke rather than a fact.

In the league championship alone he had scored about twenty goals so far that season, six or seven more in the Cup and the European competition. I usually follow football, in fact, I would

have preferred to talk about the game, ask him questions like
any other admirer, any other fan. But he must have been tired
of all that.

"Were you always like that? When you were in Hungary, at
Honved?" He had been signed up from that team in Budapest,
where he'd been born.

"Oh no, not in Hungary," he said seriously. "I had a girlfriend
there."

"And what happened to her?" I asked.

"She writes to me," he said succinctly and without the glimmer
of a smile.

"And you?"

"I never open her letters."

Szentkuthy was about twenty-three then, a boy, I was amazed
that he would have the strength of will, or the absence of curiosity necessary to do such a thing. Even if you knew the probable
content of those letters, it would be difficult not to want to know
how it was phrased. You'd have to be quite hard.

"Why? And she still writes to you despite that?"

"Yes," he replied, as if there were nothing strange about it.
"She loves me. I don't have time for her, but she doesn't understand that."

"What doesn't she understand?"

"She sees things in terms of for ever, she doesn't understand
that things change, she doesn't understand why I don't keep the
promises I made her one day, years ago."

"Promises of eternal love."

"Yes, who hasn't made promises like that, but nobody actually
keeps them. We all talk a lot, women make you talk, that's why
I learned the language here so quickly, they always want you to
talk, especially afterwards, I prefer not to say anything afterwards,
or before, like in football, you score a goal and you let out a

yell, there's no need to say or promise anything, people know you'll score more goals, and that's all there is to it. She doesn't understand, she thinks I'm hers, for ever. She's very young."

"Perhaps she'll learn with time, then."

"No, I don't think so, you don't know her. As far as she's concerned, I will always be hers, *always*."

He said that last word in an ominous, respectful tone, that "always" which was not his but hers, and which he denied every day by his actions and by the distance he had placed between them, as if that "always" nevertheless had more force than any of his denials, than any of his goals for Madrid and his volatile, interchangeable women. As if he knew that one can do nothing against an affirmative will, when your own will merely faffs around and says no, people convince themselves that they want something as a more efficient means of getting it, and those people will always have the edge over those who don't know what they want or only know what they don't want. Those of us in the latter group are defenceless, we are afflicted with an extraordinary weakness of which we are not always aware and so we can easily be destroyed by a stronger force that has chosen us, and from which we only temporarily escape, there are forces which are infinitely determined and infinitely patient. From the way Szentkuthy had said the word "always", I knew that he would end up marrying the young woman who wrote to him from his own country, I didn't think this with any particular intensity at the time, indeed it was just a circumstantial, anecdotal thought, I really didn't care, I would only see Szentkuthy after that on the television or in the stadium, as often as I could, to be sure, I loved the way he played.

Some of the dancers were returning to the table, so I said to him:

"Watch out, Kentucky, one of the three women you haven't yet had is coming home with me tonight."

He let out a loud, elemental guffaw that superimposed itself
on the music and then he returned to the dance floor. From there,
before he began dancing again, he shouted:

"And she's yours, is she? Yours for ever!"

She wasn't, but she and I left before he had exhausted his
extra time on the dance floor and found out whether that night
he would have a change of partner or be forced to repeat himself.
That afternoon he had scored three goals against Valencia. I
thought for a moment of his compatriot Kocsis, an inside-forward
for Barcelona who, I believe, bore the nickname "Goldilocks", he
committed suicide years ago, some time after retiring. I don't
know why I thought of him and not of Kubala or Puskas, who
knew how to have a good time and went on to have careers as
trainers. At least that night Szentkuthy was having a good time.

I saw him play for two more seasons, in which he had some
ups and downs, but he left behind him some indelible images.
The one that stays in my mind is the one that must stay in everyone's: in a European Cup match against Inter of Milan, in which
one goal was needed to reach the semi-finals, there were only
ten or twelve minutes left when Szentkuthy got the ball in his
half of the pitch after a corner rebounded off his own goal. He
was left alone to mount the counterattack, there were two strag-
gling defenders between him and the opposition's goalkeeper;
he outran one and dodged the other before reaching the goal
area; the goalkeeper ran desperately out to meet him, Szentkuthy
swerved past him as well, avoiding the penalty the latter tried to
force on him; then he looked at the empty goal, all he had to do
was kick the ball from the edge of the area in order to score the
goal that the whole stadium could already see and was waiting
for with that remnant of anxiety that always exists between what
is imminent and certain and its actual occurrence. The murmur
of excitement became sudden silence, concealing a cry that lay

unuttered in a hundred thousand throats: "Shoot, for God's sake, shoot now!", once the ball was in the net, everything would be certain, but not before, we had to see it in the net. Szentkuthy didn't shoot, though, he simply continued moving towards the goal with the ball glued to his foot, under control, as far as the goal line and then he stopped the ball with the sole of his boot. For a second, he held it still, captive beneath his boot on the grass or the chalk line, not letting it go over. Another two Italian defenders were racing towards him, as was the now recovered goalkeeper. They couldn't possibly get there in time, Szentkuthy only had to push it across the line, but in football, nothing is certain until it happens. I can't remember a more suffocating silence in a stadium. It was only a second but I don't think a single one of those spectators will ever forget it. It pointed out the gulf between what is unavoidable and what has not been avoided, between what is still future and what is already past, between "might be" and "was", a palpable transition which we only very rarely witness. As the goalkeeper and the two defenders hurled themselves on him, Szentkuthy rolled the ball an inch or so forward and then stopped it again once it was over the goal line. He didn't send it flying into the back of the net, he pushed it just far enough forward so that what might be a goal was one. Never has the invisible wall that stands before every goal been made so manifest. It was an act of disdain and insolence, the whole stadium went wild and was filled with waving handkerchiefs, it was a combination of admiration for his actual play and a sense of relief after the unnecessary suffering Szentkuthy had inflicted on a hundred thousand people and on the several million more who had lived through it in their homes. The radio commentators were forced to postpone their cry of "Goal", they only gave it when he wanted them to, not a second before. He had thwarted imminence, and it was not so much that he had stopped time as that he had set a mark on it and made it uncertain, as if he were saying: "I am the instigator and it will happen when I say it will happen, not when you want it. If it does happen, it is because I have decided that it should." You can't think about what would have happened if the goalkeeper had arrived in time and grabbed the ball from beneath his boot. You can't think about that because it didn't happen and because it's too terrifying, no one forgives anyone who toys with luck if luck then turns its back on him as a punishment, having, until then, been entirely in his favour. Any other player would have shot at the empty goal from the edge of the goal area when there were no further obstacles, showing a positive will to win the qualifying round and to win it as soon as possible. Szentkuthy's will was, at the very least, vacillating, as if he wanted to emphasize that nothing is inevitable: it's going to be a goal, but look, it could just as easily not be.

But it was not a good season for his team despite that game or perhaps because of it, and the season after that was disastrous. Szentkuthy seemed bored, he barely scored any goals and only played occasionally, he was injured in January and didn't recover for the whole of the rest of the championship, he hardly appeared at all.

On one occasion I was invited to watch a game from the President's box, and Szentkuthy happened to be sitting to my left; on his left was a young woman with a rather old-fashioned look about her, I heard them speaking in Hungarian, at least I assumed it was Hungarian, I didn't understand a word. Needless to say, he didn't recognize me, he scarcely looked at me, he was absorbed in the game, as if he were there on the pitch with his colleagues, tense and alert. Sometimes he would shout to them in Spanish because, from where he was sitting, he had a clear view of what they had to do at each lost opportunity. It was obviously painful to him not to be down there with them. When the goals were over, he would only have women, I thought. When he retired, he would still be too young.

At half-time, he returned to reality, but he didn't move from his place despite the cold, sunny afternoon. It was then that I dared to speak to him. He was better dressed, with a tie and an overcoat with the collar turned up, he had seen more advertisements by then; he smoked one cigarette in each half, in front of his bosses and the cameras.

"When will we see you back on the pitch, Kentucky?" I asked him.

"*Two* weeks," he said, and he raised two fingers as if to confirm the fact with a deed. It was the month of February.

The young woman, who obviously knew little Spanish, but enough to understand that, made a doubtful face, gave a modest smile and raised three fingers, then a fourth, as if reminding him of the truth of the matter. Her intervention allowed me to ask him:

"Is the young lady Hungarian too?"

"Yes, she is," he said, "but she's not my young lady." He had the literalness of someone speaking a language not his own. "She's my fiancée."

"Pleased to meet you," I said, and I held out my hand and added my name, introducing myself, this time with no mention of my profession.

"Delighted to meet you, sir," she said hesitantly, perhaps an odd phrase learned out of context, the way you immediately learn how to say "goodbye" and "thank you". She said nothing more, she sat back again in her seat, staring ahead, at the packed and rather drowsy stadium on that Sunday afternoon. It would be rash of me to say anything about her, I only saw her in profile and I heard her say still less. Just that she was very young and quite attractive, with an air about her that was at once shy and determined, an affirmative will. She was nothing special compared to the girls at the Joy discotheque, not even compared to the woman who went home with me that night, I hadn't seen her for a while, perhaps they had met again, Szentkuthy and her, at another night of partying when it would no longer have mattered to me who she went with. I know nothing about his fiancée and I knew little enough then, that afternoon in the Presidential box.

The game was drawn nil-nil and the team was playing badly, they were keen but uninspired. On days like that Szentkuthy was sorely missed, although up until he was injured, he hadn't exactly shone.

"So, how do you think this is going to end?" I asked.

He looked at me with an air of momentary superiority, probably because I was asking his opinion, but I've often noticed that look in recently married men, although he had not yet married. Sometimes it's the expression of an attempt at respectability that philanderers might make in order to flatter their wives or fiancées when they've just got married or are about to do so. Later they abandon it, the attempt.

"Win easy, lose difficult."

I didn't quite understand what he meant and I sat thinking about it during the second half. If they won, they would do so easily; if they lost, it would be with difficulty; or else, it would be easy for them to win and difficult for them to lose, perhaps that was it, impossible to know. He was in no mood for chatting and I didn't want to insist. He immediately turned back to his girl-friend, they talked together in Hungarian, almost in a whisper. She was one of those women who attracts the attention of her husband or fiancé by tugging at his sleeve with two fingers or by slipping her hand into his overcoat pocket, I couldn't explain it any other way, nor should I.

In the second half they won three-nil and, for the most part, the team played very well from then on. So they scarcely missed Szentkuthy. His knee injury was much worse than he had thought at first, much worse than he had thought in February and in March and in April and in May. Or rather he did not respond well to his convalescence after the operation. He had some conflicts with the trainer and at the end of the season, the club sacked him, he moved to a French club, which is where great players go when it looks like they're not going to be quite as great as expected and won't be remembered as such. He played for three more years in Nantes, to little effect, we didn't hear much about him here, journalists soon forget, so much so that news of his death only appeared in any detail in the sporting press which I don't usually buy, a nephew of mine showed me a cutting. Szentkuthy left Madrid eight years ago, he probably hadn't played football for five of those years, unless he had done the rounds of the less famous teams in his own country, here hardly anyone knows anything about Hungary. He was thirty-three at the time of his death, a young man with no new goals and with videos that were now old hat could only collect women in his native Budapest, there he would still be an idol, the boy who left and triumphed in a far-off land and who would live for ever off the proud memory of his distant, fast-fading adventures. He's not alive because he was shot in the chest, and perhaps there was a second when his timid, determined wife's affirmative will weakened and she hesitated before squeezing the hard trigger with her two frail fingers, although, at the same time, she knew she would do it. Perhaps there was a second when imminence was thwarted and time was marked and became uncertain, and during which Szentkuthy clearly saw the dividing line and the normally invisible wall that separates life and death, the only "might be" and the only "was" that count, and these are sometimes controlled by the most trivial things, by two feeble fingers that have grown tired of slipping into a pocket or tugging at a sleeve, tired of being beneath the sole of a boot.

NO MORE LOVE

IT IS QUITE possible that the main aim of ghosts, if they still exist, is to thwart the desires of mortal tenants, appearing if their presence is unwelcome and hiding away if it is expected or demanded. Sometimes, however, agreements have been reached, as we know from various documents collected by Lord Halifax and Lord Rymer in the 1930s.

One of the most modest and touching of these cases is that of an old lady living in Rye, around 1910: a suitable place for such enduring relationships, since both Henry James and E. F. Benson lived in Rye for some years and in the same house, Lamb House (each at different times, Benson even became mayor), two writers who most assiduously and successfully occupied themselves with such visits and expectations, or, perhaps, nostalgias. In her youth, this old lady (Molly Morgan Muir was her name) was companion to a wealthy, older lady, to whom, amongst other services rendered, she used to read novels out loud in order to ease the tedium of the older lady's lack of requirements and of an early, unavoidable widowhood: according to people in the town, Mrs Cromer-Blake had suffered the occasional illicit disappointment in love after her brief marriage, and it was probably this – rather

than the death of her slightly or entirely unmemorable husband –
that had made her seem harsh and withdrawn at an age when
those characteristics in a woman are no longer intriguing or
charming or the object of jokes. Boredom made her so lazy that
she was barely able to read by herself, in silence, alone, and so
she had her companion read out loud to her details of affairs
and feelings which, with each day that passed – and they passed
very quickly and monotonously – seemed more and more
removed from that house. The lady always listened very silently,
utterly absorbed, and only occasionally asked Molly Morgan
Muir to repeat a passage or a dialogue to which she did not wish
to bid farewell for ever without, first, making some attempt to
hold on to it. When Molly finished reading, her only remark
would be: "Molly, you have a lovely voice. You will find love
with that voice."

And it was during these sessions that the ghost of the house
made his appearance: every evening, while Molly was speaking
the words of Stevenson or Jane Austen or Dumas or Conan
Doyle, she could just make out the figure of a young man, of
rustic appearance, a stable lad. The first time she saw him, standing, leaning his elbows on the back of the chair occupied by the
lady, as if he were listening intently to the text she was reading,
she almost cried out with fright. But the young man immediately
raised a forefinger to his lips and made reassuring signs to her
indicating that she should continue and not betray his presence.
He had such an inoffensive face, and a constant, shy smile in his
mocking eyes that occasionally gave way, during certain sombre
passages, to the alarmed, ingenuous seriousness of someone
who cannot quite distinguish between what is real and what is
imagined. The young woman obeyed, although that first day,
she could not help glancing up rather too frequently and looking
over the bun on top of the head of Mrs Cromer-Blake, who also

kept glancing up, as if wondering if some hypothetical hat were awry or if her halo were not bright enough. "What's wrong, girl?" she said, annoyed. "What is it you keep looking at up there?" "Nothing," said Molly Muir, "it's just a way of resting my eyes before going back to the text. Reading for such a long time tires my eyes." The young man with the scarf about his neck nodded and the explanation meant that the young woman could thereafter continue the habit and thus at least satisfy her visual curiosity. For, from then on, evening after evening and with very few exceptions, she read for her lady and also for him, without the lady ever once turning round or discovering the young man's intrusive presence.

The young man did not linger or appear at any other moment, so Molly Muir never had the opportunity, over the years, of speaking to him or asking who he was or had been or why he was listening to her. She considered the possibility that he might have been the cause of the illicit disappointment in love suffered by her lady at some time in the past, but her lady never offered any confidences, despite the insinuations made by all those pages read out loud and by Molly herself during the slow, nocturnal conversations of half a lifetime. Perhaps the rumour was false and the lady had nothing worth telling, which was why she asked to hear about the most remote and foreign and improbable of tales. On more than one occasion, Molly was tempted to be kind and to tell her what was going on each evening behind her back, to allow her to share her small daily excitement, to tell her of the existence of a man between those ever more asexual, taciturn walls in which there was only the echo, sometimes for whole nights and days together, of their feminine voices, the lady's grown ever older and more confused, and Molly Muir's, each morning, a little less beautiful, weaker and more fugitive, and which, contrary to the predictions, had not brought her love, at least not a love that would stay, that could be touched. But whenever she was about to give in to that temptation, she would suddenly remember the young man's discreet gesture – his forefinger on his lips, repeated now and then with a slightly teasing look in his eyes – and so she kept silent. The last thing she wanted was to make him angry. Perhaps ghosts got as bored as widows did.

When Mrs Cromer-Blake died, Molly stayed on in the house, and for a few days, saddened and disoriented, she stopped reading: the young man did not appear. Convinced that the young country lad wanted to have the education he had doubtless lacked in life, but also fearful that this was not the case and that his presence had been mysteriously linked with the old lady alone, she decided to go back to reading out loud in order to call him back, and she read not only novels, but books on history and the natural sciences. The young man took some while to reappear – perhaps ghosts go into mourning, for they have more reason to than anyone else – but he finally did, perhaps drawn by the new material, which he continued listening to with the same close attention, not standing up this time, leaning on the back of the chair, but comfortably seated in the now vacant armchair, sometimes with his legs crossed and holding a lit pipe in his hand, like the patriarch he never became.

The young woman, who was growing older, spoke ever more confidingly to him, but without ever getting a reply: ghosts cannot always speak nor do they always want to. And as that unilateral trust grew, so the years passed, until one day the boy failed to appear, nor did he appear in the days and weeks that followed. The young woman, who was now almost old, was worried at first like a mother, fearing that some grave accident or misfortune might have befallen him, without realizing that things only happen to mortals, that those who are not are safe. When she understood this, her worry turned to desperation: evening after evening, she would stare at the empty armchair and curse the silence, she would ask sorrowful questions of the void, hurl reproaches into the invisible air, she wondered what mistake or error she could have made and she searched eagerly for new texts that might arouse the young man's curiosity and make him come back, new disciplines and new novels, and she awaited avidly each new instalment of Sherlock Holmes, for she put more faith in his skill and lyricism than in any other scientific or literary bait. She continued to read out loud every day, to see if he would come.

One evening, after months of desolation, she found that the bookmark she had left in the Dickens she was patiently reading to him in his absence was not where she had left it, but many pages ahead. She carefully read the pages he had marked, and then, bitterly, she understood and she suffered the disappointment that comes in every life, however recondite and still that life might be. There was a sentence in the text that said: "And she grew old and lined, and her cracked voice was no longer pleasing to him." Lord Rymer says that the old lady became as indignant as a rejected wife, and that, far from accepting this judgement and falling silent, she addressed the void most reproachfully: "You are unfair. You do not grow old and you want pleasant, youthful voices, you wish to contemplate firm, luminous faces. Don't think I don't understand you, you're young and you always will be. But I have educated and amused you for years, if, thanks to me, you have learned many things, including how to read, it was not so that now you could leave me offensive messages via the very texts I have always shared with you. Bear in mind that when the old lady died, I could easily have read in silence, but I didn't. I know that you can go in search of other voices, nothing binds you to me and it's true that you've never asked me for anything, so you owe me nothing. But if you have any notion of gratitude, I ask you to come at least once a week to listen to me and to have patience with my voice, which is no longer a beautiful voice and no longer pleases you, because now it will never bring me love. I will try hard and continue reading as well as I can. But do come, because now that I'm old, it is I who need you to amuse me, to be here."

According to Lord Rymer, the ghost of the eternal rustic youth was not entirely lacking in understanding and he listened to reason or else understood what gratitude meant: from then on, until her death, Molly Morgan Muir awaited with excitement and impatience the arrival of the day chosen by her impalpable, silent love to return to the past of his time in which, in fact, there was no past and no time, the arrival of each Wednesday. And it is thought that that was what kept her alive for many more years, that is, with a past and a present and a future too or perhaps it was just nostalgia.